Wicked Fog

An Ivy Morgan Mystery
Book Six

Lily Harper Hart

One

The air was crisp as it whipped around Jack Harker, causing him to make a face and snuggle closer to his girlfriend as he watched the denizens of Shadow Lake bustle about the town square as they readied the annual Halloween festival.

"This bites," Jack muttered, lowering his nose to Ivy Morgan's cheek and pressing the cold protuberance to her warm skin. "How are you warm when it's so cold out?"

Ivy, her long brown hair shot through with streaks of pink, made a face. "It's sixty degrees out, Jack."

"It doesn't feel that warm," Jack complained, tightening his green army jacket around him as he regarded the feisty woman at his side. "It feels downright freezing. Let's go back to your house and start a fire. I'm convinced if we go into hibernation mode now we'll survive until spring. If we wait too long, our very survival is in jeopardy."

Jack wasn't a northern Lower Michigan native. He grew up in Detroit, making his home in the suburbs there until two gunshots to the chest ended his time with the city's police department. After recovering, he moved north because he wanted quiet and peace. What he got was Ivy Morgan, and while he ignored her pull for as long as he could – about two weeks, although she was convinced it was two hours – he ultimately lost the fight to stay away. He'd never been so happy to lose a battle. That didn't mean he liked the weather.

"I think you're just a city boy at heart," Ivy teased, poking his ribs. She didn't have a coat on, and her bohemian skirt didn't cover her feet – which were clad in sandals instead of regular shoes. "I'm a country girl at heart. Maybe we're destined for sadness."

"Oh, we're destined for something, honey, but it's not sadness," Jack said, slipping his arm around Ivy's waist and causing her to squeal as he pulled her close. "Just because I grew up in the city, though, that doesn't mean I'm a city boy. I'm pretty sure I'm a country boy."

"Then why are you complaining?"

"It's cold, honey," Jack replied, not missing a beat. "In the city it stays warmer longer."

"Jack, sixty degrees is downright balmy for this time of year," Ivy argued. "This is great weather for the Halloween festival. By the middle of November we'll probably have snow."

Jack made a disgusted face. "Snow? We don't get snow in the city until January and even then we only get three big drops a year and then it melts in between. I get the feeling you're talking about something else entirely and it makes me want to hibernate sooner rather than later."

"I'm definitely talking about something else," Ivy confirmed, slipping her arms around Jack's waist and resting her chin on his solid chest as she studied his chiseled features. She was tall for a woman, but Jack towered over her. He made her feel safe. He also made her feel loved, although the couple hadn't said those particular words to one another yet. It would happen. Ivy had faith. They'd only been together a few months, after all. They had plenty of time to build up to big declarations. That didn't mean she wasn't going to enjoy her favorite time of year with her favorite man. "Once it snows here the ground usually stays covered until spring."

Jack blew a loud raspberry as he rocked Ivy, ignoring the stares of the town folk as they hurried past to help with the festival setup. Ivy wasn't usually a joiner, so when she told him she was busy setting up the Halloween fair – and would even have her own booth to sell lotion and candles – Jack was understandably curious. He had to see it for himself.

The cold made him rethink that, although the idea of snuggling with Ivy was always welcome – even if people couldn't stop themselves from staring. "Explain this snow sticking for months at a time thing," Jack said, his tone teasing. "Does that mean we'll be officially snowed in?"

Ivy snorted. "You're a police officer. You can't be snowed in. You're always on call."

"Yes, but I'm considering quitting my job and living off the kindness of a beautiful woman," he shot back, grinning as she kissed his chin. "I'm going to let you do all of the heavy lifting this winter. I'll pick up the financial burden in the spring ... when I can feel my toes."

"Oh, you're going to be able to feel your toes," Ivy said. "That's what the fireplace is for." Her eyes sparkled as her expression shifted and took on a far-off quality. "Think about it, Jack. There are going to be days when we get a foot of snow and we're going to be able to spend forty-eight hours straight with nothing to do but drink hot chocolate and be together."

Jack hated the idea of snow, but he loved the idea of cuddling in front of a fire with Ivy. "That sounds great," he said. "Let's start doing that now."

"It's not snowing yet," Ivy pointed out. "The first snow is always magical, though. You have to promise to go for a walk with me during the first snow."

"What if it snows in the middle of the night?"

"Then we'll get up and take a walk."

Jack wrinkled his nose. "You want me to get out of a warm bed and walk with you in snow for no good reason? Are you crazy?"

"I'll make it worth your while," Ivy promised, rolling to the balls of her feet so she could kiss the ridge of his ear. "I promise it will be fun."

The sultry tone of her voice caused Jack's insides to turn to jiggling gelatin as he clutched her closer. "Oh, you could talk a snowman into a pair of snow pants," Jack murmured, making chewing noises as he kissed her neck. "I'll go for a walk with you in the snow."

"Good."

Jack knew she would get him to give in before he started arguing, but the smile she graced him with was worth all of the manipulation. "It definitely sounds good," Jack said, giving her a soft kiss before moving back far enough to sling an arm over her shoulders and stare at the town square. "What can you tell me about this shindig?"

Ivy rubbed her hands together, excited. "Well, it's always so much fun because we have a haunted corn maze and a dance. Everyone gets dressed up and we have warm cider. Oh, and there's hayrides. There's a haunted house at the carnival for the kids – but I enjoy it, too. Did I mention Halloween is my favorite time of year?"

Jack cocked an eyebrow, her enthusiasm taking him by surprise and yet warming him at the same time. She was an excitable person, but this was the first time since meeting her he could remember outright joy due to an event causing her to bubble in this manner.

"You didn't, but if you're this worked up, I have a feeling it's going to be my favorite holiday, too," Jack teased, goosing her bottom when he knew no one was looking and causing her to squeal. "I'm looking forward to filling you with treats, Ms. Morgan."

Ivy's smile was so wide it almost split her entire face. "I like licorice … and peanut butter cups … and Almond Joys, for that matter, the best."

"That's good to know," Jack said. "I'm looking forward to sugaring you up, stripping you naked, and putting a blanket on the living room floor in front of the fireplace."

Ivy's mouth dropped open at the brazen flirting. "Jack!" She feigned being scandalized. "Be careful. People might hear you."

"Ivy!" Jack mocked her tone. "I don't care who hears me. I'm happy. You're ecstatic. We don't have a murder … or a traumatized girl … or outright danger plaguing us. I want to enjoy this."

Ivy's expression softened. They had been through a lot for a "fresh" couple. The day they met it was because Ivy found a dead body in the ditch by her house. Jack was instantly drawn to her, but after his own troubles he didn't want to get involved with anyone so he fought the attraction. That turned out to be a wasted effort.

Now, after months of dating and sharing dreams with one another, Jack realized he'd never been this happy. Even before his partner turned on him and left him for dead in an alley, Jack didn't think it was possible to adore anyone as much as he adored Ivy. She made him laugh … and outright giggle sometimes … and she always made him feel content.

Shadow Lake was supposed to be a quiet place for Jack to retreat. Instead it had been a hotbed of activity – including the discovery last month of a teenaged girl held captive for a long period of time – and Jack was looking forward to a relaxing week with his girl.

"Tell me what you want me to do," Jack said. "I'll help however I can."

"You don't have to do anything," Ivy said. "We're just here for the ceremonial opening of the corn maze."

Jack glanced around, confused. "There's no corn here."

"I know that," Ivy said, rolling her eyes. She was cute and cuddly today, but her sarcasm remained intact despite the romantic overtones of the afternoon. "It's going to be held on the other side of the horse stable property."

"Oh, *that* is a cornfield," Jack said, realization dawning. "I thought those were just really tall weeds when I first moved here. I had no idea that was corn until I saw people stopping to buy bags of the stuff and take it home"

"You did not," Ivy scoffed, giggling.

"I did, too," Jack said, tugging Ivy closer. "Are you going to take me on a tour of this corn maze when it's open?"

"I am."

"Is it going to be a naughty tour?"

"It had better not be." Max Morgan, Ivy's brother, made a face as he appeared in the space next to Ivy and Jack. He was fond of his sister – in fact, they were incredibly tight – but he was also a fan of Jack and Ivy's relationship. He wanted his sister to be happy. He just didn't want to hear about their sex life if he could help it. "This is a family-friendly event. You guys cannot be gross in public. The Morgan family will never live it down if you do."

Jack pursed his lips, scorching Max with a dark look as he kept his hand on Ivy's waist. "You saw we were busy, right?"

"I did," Max confirmed. "I saw your dirty lips all over my sister."

"So why did you come over here to interrupt us?" Jack asked.

"Because the opening of the corn maze is an annual event," Max replied.

"I figured," Jack said. "I've never seen this many people downtown ... well, except for when they host those weird dance things in the barn. Then there are a lot of people down here, too."

"You didn't let me finish," Max said. "The corn maze opening is an annual event ... and Ivy and go to it together. We make a day of it. We bob for apples ... and drink cider ... and frolic in the falling leaves."

"Oh." Jack's heart sank. The last thing he wanted was to come between Ivy and her brother. "I didn't realize you guys had a regular date. I can keep myself entertained."

Max snorted as Ivy shot her brother a dirty look.

"Don't listen to him," Ivy said. "We most certainly don't frolic in the leaves and I'm not a big fan of bobbing for anything because I hate germs. I invited you here because I want you with me. Yes, it's true Max and I come to the opening together every year, but that's only because he wants to check out the haystack honeys – that's his term, not mine, by the way – and I'm a convenient excuse for him not to have to attend alone."

That was a lot of information for Jack to absorb all at once. "Haystack honeys?"

"I knew that would be the thing to pique your interest," Ivy grumbled, fighting the urge to smile when Jack poked her side.

"You're the only woman I care about, haystack or otherwise, honey," Jack said, grinning. "As for you … ." He narrowed his eyes as he regarded Max.

"Fine, you can come with us," Max said. "It's important that you stick close to Ivy, though. The women who run the corn maze dress up in low-cut tops and wear their hair in pigtails. They're adorable … and sexy. They'll take one look at you and forget about me if I'm not careful, though.

"So, while we're there, we need rules," he continued. "You fawn over Ivy and make all of the women make that 'aw' sound because they want a man to look at them the way you look at my sister – don't take it too far and be gross, though. Then I shall swoop in and sweep them off their feet when they're at their most vulnerable."

Jack ran his tongue over his teeth as he regarded Max. He liked the gregarious man a great deal, but he wasn't thrilled at being used as a virtual wingman. "Why would I do that?"

"Because I let you sleep with my sister and don't put up a fuss," Max replied, not missing a beat. "I have a key to her house and an open invitation to raid the refrigerator. I could make life very difficult for you."

Jack refused to be pushed around. "I don't care. Come over whenever you want. I have no problem being naked in front of you."

"Ivy!" Max took on a whiny tone. "He's grossing me out."

"You're grossing me out," Ivy shot back, her forehead creasing. "Why can't you meet a nice woman and settle down? How come you're always on the prowl for haystack honeys ... and Christmas cupids ... and those horrible spring succubi?"

"Wow," Jack intoned, shaking his head. "I cannot believe you came up with all of those names."

"It wasn't hard," Max said. "I bore easily and my phone has a built-in Thesaurus. As for the rest of what you said, Ivy, I happen to be happy with my lot in life. Not all of us are meant for one woman."

"Oh, you don't know what you're missing," Jack said, pulling Ivy a tad closer as he kissed her cheek. "My one woman takes up more energy than ten of yours do."

"I'm also smarter than all ten of them combined," Ivy added.

Jack bobbed his head. "That, too."

"Yes, you clearly know the way to my heart," Max deadpanned. "I love a good scientific debate before I roll in the hay with a hot honey."

"You're a sick man," Jack said, although he didn't appear particularly bothered. "I will gladly shower your sister with affection and ship all of the nostalgic women in your direction when they see me fawning all over her. Are you happy?"

"Thrilled."

"Then let's go," Jack said, linking his fingers with Ivy's and giving her a good tug. "This town never ceases to amaze me with the weird crap they come up with to entertain everyone. I've never seen a corn maze, and I have no intention of missing this one."

"Let's go," Ivy said, beaming. "Did I mention this is my favorite time of year?"

"Only about a hundred times, honey," Jack said. "I'll never grow tired of hearing it as long as you tell me the tale with that smile."

"Consider it done."

"Oh, be still my heart," Jack teased, grinning.

"Yes, and be still my lunch so I don't throw it up," Max complained. "Come on. I want you two to put on a show before all of that sappy love talk oozes out and you start fighting … as you inevitably always do."

"That shows how much you know," Ivy said. "We've decided not to fight this week."

Max snorted. Ivy and Jack were known for their passionate arguing skills. "And I've got twenty bucks that says you won't last a day before that falls by the wayside."

"You're on."

Two

"Wow."

Jack's face lit up when he turned the corner behind the stable and he saw the decked-out cornfield. Workers were busy setting up the maze, the sound of weed whackers echoing from deep inside the field, and every inch of space close to the opening was decorated with orange and black party favors.

"Isn't it fun?" Ivy rubbed her hands together as she studied the garish Halloween tableau at the opening of the maze. "Did I mention I love Halloween?"

"Just a few times, honey," Jack said, tilting his head to the side. He'd honestly never seen her this excited. He wasn't complaining – he loved her smile, after all – but he wasn't sure how to respond. "Can I ask what this delightful holiday attitude stems from?"

"I just like the holiday," Ivy said hurriedly, averting her gaze. Jack didn't believe her for a second. "I'm going to grab some cider before they do the ribbon cutting. I'll be right back." She darted away before Jack could press her further, leaving the befuddled man to shift his attention to Max.

"Don't look at me," Max said, offering a saucy wink to one of the blondes dressing the skeleton at the corner of the maze. "I am loyal to my sister. Where she is concerned, my lips are zipped."

Jack flicked Max's ear and leveled him with a serious gaze. "Talk."

"Okay, you tortured me into it," Max said, sighing. "I'm only telling you because Ivy is so ridiculously happy. I don't want you to accidentally ruin it by ... I don't know ... breaking her heart."

Jack was confused. "And how would I do that?"

"I don't know," Max replied, making a face. "Just don't break up with her or anything. That would forever ruin Halloween, and that's the only time she's pleasant to be around."

"You take that back," Jack ordered, catching Max off guard. "She's always pleasant to be around."

"Oh, I don't even know why I said that," Max said, offering Jack an exaggerated eye roll. "You're too smitten to ever break up with her. You're her willing sex slave ... her love monkey, if you will."

"Don't ever call me her 'love monkey' again," Jack warned.

"What about the sex slave part?"

"I'm fine with that."

"You're so sick," Max complained. "As for the Halloween thing, I don't know how to explain it. She's always been in love with the holiday. She likes the changing of the leaves and she loves pumpkin-flavored everything. She's also a big fan of horror movies and storms."

"I know about the storms," Jack said. "The first time we had a big thunderstorm it rocked that small house and I thought it was going to fall down around us, but she couldn't stop herself from hopping around and staring out each window."

"Yes, well, my sister is multifaceted weird," Max said, his eyes momentarily sobering. "In truth, Ivy was kind of a lonely kid. The other kids thought she was weird – and rightly so, because there are many times I think she's bonkers – but when you live in a small town like this the inclination is to shun anyone who doesn't fit into a mold."

"That's the only thing I hate about this place," Jack mused, rubbing his chin. "She's kind of isolated. She spends all of her time with you and me. She never tries to smother me, though. When I want to go fishing she waves and sends me off. She's happy with her own company, which is one of the things I like best about her."

"Oh, you smitten kitten," Max said, smirking as he poked Jack's cheek and earned a scowl. "She is fine on her own. That doesn't mean I don't think she would do good with a female friend. I'm not sure it's healthy to spend all of her time with you and me."

"Especially you," Jack intoned.

"Especially you," Max shot back, although his grin was impish instead of mean. "The only time Ivy was happy to hang around with other kids when we were growing up was close to Halloween."

"But why?"

"I think it's because she could dress up and be anyone she wanted to be," Max replied. "I mean, she never dressed up as anyone but herself, but her skirts and wild hair fit in around Halloween. Plus, as she got older, the guys started to realize that being different was cool and they threw themselves at her feet.

"The only dance Ivy was interested in attending was the Halloween one," he continued. "She had a lot of suitors. For that week, she was the center of attention and didn't shrink from it. I don't know how to explain it."

"Well, I could've done without the suitors tidbit," Jack said. "As for the rest … I wish she wasn't so self-conscious."

"She's not really self-conscious," Max clarified. "I mean, she knows people stare at her and everything, don't get me wrong, but it's not about being self-conscious. She was that way when she was a kid, but when she grew up she learned to tune it out. She honestly doesn't care what people think about her."

"I like that about her, too," Jack said. "I still don't like her feeling isolated. Everyone should look at her and think she's the greatest woman in the world … because she is."

"Oh, you are sappy and schmaltzy and I kind of want to hug you anyway," Max said, shaking his head. "You're the best thing that's ever happened to my sister. I'm uttering it out loud, but if you ever tell anyone I said it, I'll be forced to beat you up."

Jack snorted. He wasn't worried in the least about Max backing up that threat. "She's the best thing that ever happened to me."

"And that's why I don't even care about the filthy things you two are doing together," Max teased. "Just enjoy the season, Jack. She won't stay this way forever. She's happy. You guys should be happy together."

"She's excited for winter, too, though," Jack argued. "She just told me she wants to take a walk during the first snow."

"Yeah, well, that's a different story," Max said. "She says she's excited now, but that will last exactly two weeks until she ends up spun out in a ditch or starts going stir-crazy because she can't walk in the woods. And just wait until she slips on the ice and blames you for not chipping every bit of it off the front porch. Look out when that happens."

"But … she said she loved it," Jack protested.

"She always says that and then turns on the season the second the going gets rough," Max said. "Good luck with that, by the way. You're on driveway duty this year. That's another bonus for me. You can shovel her out."

"Screw shoveling her out," Jack countered. "I'm looking forward to being snowed in."

Max grinned. "That's a nice way of looking at it."

"She's nice to look at," Jack teased, shifting his eyes back to the maze. "Where the heck did she go, by the way?"

"I don't know," Max answered. "Let's find her, shall we? It will allow me the chance to get a gander at this year's honeys without being overtly lecherous."

"Yes, that is important," Jack deadpanned. "You're kind of a pig. You know that, right?"

"I can live with that."

JACK found himself on edge as he looked for Ivy. It wasn't that he thought a corn maze was especially dangerous – although he'd seen enough horror movies to know that it could be creepy and potentially evil if small children decided to start doing away with adults – but the idea of Ivy disappearing bothered him.

They'd suffered through more trouble than was fair since getting together, and yet they'd come out the other side stronger. He knew Ivy could take care of herself. That didn't mean he wanted her wandering around a corn maze without him.

"Where is she?"

"Chill out, drama queen," Max intoned, scanning the crowd. "Ivy has been taking care of herself for a really long time. She's getting cider. That doesn't generally end in bloodshed."

"Ha, ha," Jack drawled, scorching Max with a harsh look. "Don't make jokes about your sister getting hurt. I don't like it."

"Oh, you're so whipped," Max said. "I … there she is." Despite his bravado, he almost seemed relieved as he pointed.

Jack followed Max's finger with his gaze and felt his heart warm when he caught sight of Ivy. The feeling only lasted until he saw the frown on her face. She listened as a middle-aged man chatted, two mugs of hot cider clutched in her hands, but she didn't look happy with the new development.

"Who is that?" Jack asked, rubbing the back of his neck. He didn't recognize the man talking Ivy's ear off.

"That's Mitch Danes," Max replied, knitting his eyebrows together. "He's a local guy we've known forever."

"Ivy doesn't seem to like him."

"Ivy doesn't like anyone but you," Max countered. "As for Mitch, well, he's harmless enough. He's got a bit of a reputation as a tool – especially when it comes to women – but I've never heard of him being grabby or anything."

"I wasn't worried about that," Jack said. "Well, I wasn't worried about that until now," he hurriedly corrected. "I just wanted to know who he is. Ivy looks as if she wants to run."

"That's probably because Mitch is a politician," Max explained. "He's running for mayor in the upcoming election."

"Oh." Things slid into place for Jack ."I knew that name sounded familiar. Brian mentioned it the other day. This is the guy running on a public safety platform, right?"

"Yeah. He runs on the very same platform every four years," Max said. "He's a local farmer who fancies himself a great leader. He runs for mayor every four years … and loses every four years."

"The mayor's name is Spinks, right? I've never actually met him even though he technically signs my paycheck every two weeks."

"Yeah, Wilford Spinks," Max said. "He's been mayor since I was a kid. He's friendly with the older crowd like Mom and Dad – and probably Brian, for that matter – but I've never had occasion to spend much time with him."

Brian Nixon was Jack's partner and the father of one of Max's longtime pals. Jack enjoyed having Brian's wisdom when it came to the town, but he had serious doubts his partner would appreciate Max considering him part of the "older crowd."

As if reading his mind, Max scowled. "Don't tell Brian I said that."

"I wouldn't dream of it," Jack said, although he didn't sound very convincing. "I mean … you're practically family, Max. I would never turn against you."

"You suck," Max muttered, his eyes flashing. "Do you know what? I bought a package of gummy witches at a specialty store the other day. I was going to surprise Ivy with them. They're black licorice flavored – which is her favorite – and I'll give them to you if you promise not to tell Brian."

Jack pursed his lips. "Deal."

The ease at which Jack acquiesced made Max suspicious. "You weren't going to tell him anyway, were you?"

"Probably not," Jack answered. "It's too late to take it back, though. I want that candy for my girl."

"You're so gross," Max grumbled, scuffing his foot on the grass as he shifted his eyes back to Ivy. "We should probably save her. She looks as if she wants to throw that cider on him rather than listen to another second of his campaign pitch."

"Let's save my damsel," Jack said, grinning as he moved in Ivy's direction. The second their eyes locked she looked as if she was going to jump him right then and there she was so relieved to have a distraction. "Hello, honey. I got worried when you didn't return."

Ivy forced a smile for Jack's benefit as she handed him a mug of cider. "This is Mitch Danes. He's running for mayor."

"Oh, well, how nice to meet you," Jack said, keeping his tone amiable as he extended his hand and greeted Mitch. "I'm still getting to know faces in town, but I'm happy to meet you."

Max glanced between Jack and Ivy's hands and made a pitiful expression. "Where is my cider?"

"I only have two hands," Ivy said.

"Yes, but … you've known me much longer than Jack," Max said. "I deserve dibs on the cider. This is our outing, after all. He's an interloper."

"Here," Jack said, licking the lip of his cup. "You can have mine."

"Oh, that was such a loser move," Max said, annoyed when Ivy giggled. "I thought I missed all the cup-licking times because I had a sister. Who knew I was going to have to put up with it in my twenties?"

"You're almost thirty," Ivy interjected.

"And now I hate you, too," Max said, horrified. "My life sucks!"

"And you say I'm dramatic," Jack said, shaking his head before focusing on Mitch again. "Are you having a nice day at the maze?"

"I'm here to make people aware that I'm the best candidate for the mayoral job," Mitch countered, refusing to indulge in small talk. "I was just explaining to young Ivy that, as a woman, she's especially vulnerable should someone want to harm her."

"And I explained to Mitch that just because I'm a woman, that doesn't mean I'm helpless," Ivy said. "He didn't seem to agree with me."

"Well, I can vouch for her not being helpless," Max said. "She once pinched my nipple so hard it turned purple – and not like a cool purple. She bites when you try to put her head in your armpit, too."

Jack had to press his lips together to keep from laughing. Max tossed out the information as if he was saying he bought iceberg lettuce instead of romaine – which was a big no-no in Ivy's house – but Mitch apparently didn't find him at all funny.

"I don't think you'd be so blasé if someone broke into your sister's home and raped her," Mitch said.

"Hey!" Jack was officially annoyed, and Mitch had the good sense to shrink back when he saw the anger on the big man's face. "Don't say things like that."

"I was just making an observation," Mitch said nervously.

"Well, don't," Jack said. "I don't like it."

"I'm perfectly safe in my home because Jack is always there," Ivy said, taking pity on Mitch. "I promise I'm okay."

"She has an attack cat, too," Max added, hoping to alleviate the tension. "She's fine. Jack is big and mean and growls like a caveman when he clubs my sister over the head and drags her toward the bedroom."

"Max!" Ivy was mortified, her cheeks turning a mottled shade of red.

"You'll live," Max said. "Personally, I think Mitch has a point about crime. I think we need more focus on keeping people safe. With that in mind, I think I should offer my burly shoulders to that haystack honey over yonder. She looks positively frightened without me to watch over her."

Ivy made a face. "You're so gross."

"I just told your boyfriend the same thing because he gets a moony look whenever your name pops up," Max said. "Somehow I think we'll all survive the mutual grossness."

"I'm not sure you'll survive," Jack countered. "As for the rest … ."

Whatever he was about to say was cut short because a terrified scream broke free from the field, causing everyone milling about in front of the entrance to snap their heads in that direction. Jack didn't immediately race into the field so he could investigate the noise because he wasn't certain someone wasn't screwing around – or perhaps playing a rousing game of hide the corncob behind the tall stalks. He honestly didn't know what to think, so he waited a beat.

"What the … ?"

A second scream filled the air, and this time Jack was certain this was no game and the stakes were real.

"Come on, honey," he said, grabbing Ivy's hand. "We have to see what's going on and I refuse to leave you behind."

Three

Jack kept a firm grip on Ivy's hand. In truth, he knew it would've been easier to leave her behind while checking out the source of the scream. He also knew curiosity was one of her biggest weaknesses (while also being a true strength) and she wouldn't be able to refrain from checking out things on her own. He figured it would be easier to keep her with him from the start rather than risk losing sight of her in the miles of cornstalks.

"Which way?" Ivy asked, tilting her head to the side. "I'm not sure which direction the scream came from other than out there somewhere."

"I know," Jack said, licking his lips. "I … ."

Another scream propelled them forward, and even though Ivy boasted long legs, she had trouble keeping up with Jack when he began running again. She tried to wrench her hand free in an effort to clear him to move ahead without her, but he fought the effort.

"It's okay, Jack," Ivy prodded. "I'll be right behind you."

"I'll slow down," Jack said, shaking his head. "I'm sorry."

"Go." Ivy wasn't one to wilt under pressure, and today was no exception. "I'll be okay."

Jack made a face. "Someone is screaming in a cornfield and we're running toward potential trouble," he argued. "I know you're going to be okay, because I'm going to keep you with me and make sure you're okay."

Now it was Ivy's turn to scowl. "You're so bossy."

"Look who is talking," Jack grumbled, tugging her arm and encouraging her to pick up the pace. "Come on, honey. You're staying with me and I don't have time to argue."

"You're kind of a pain. You know that, right?"

"I'm fairly certain we're pains together," Jack countered. "That's just the way we roll."

Despite the serious nature of the situation, Ivy couldn't help but smirk. When another loud noise – this one more of an excited utterance full of obscenities instead of a scream – filled the air, the couple put their petty bickering aside for the time being. They both knew they would revisit the minor argument later.

"I think it's this way," Ivy said, changing their direction slightly and choosing a fork in the maze that led to the west. "In years past, the center of the maze was down this route. They have a big clearing there with a dark fantasy scene. They throw a big party there Halloween night so all of the ghosts and goblins have everyone together in one place when they're ready for some thrills and chills."

"Do I even want to know what that means?"

Jack wasn't directionally challenged, but he never second-guessed Ivy's instincts. She always seemed to know exactly where they should be and he wasn't so alpha that he couldn't acquiesce to her special abilities. The dream walking was only a fraction of the magic that seemed to surround her, and Jack was convinced she was growing in power – even though he was reluctant to admit it to her because she seemed somehow embarrassed or worried by his observations.

"Here."

Ivy and Jack plowed through the small opening and found themselves in the middle of a wide clearing. Jack sucked in several deep breaths to calm himself as he glanced around. He couldn't help but notice that Ivy didn't even seem out of breath, which was somewhat annoying considering she hardly ever worked out.

"Maisie?" Ivy was confused when her gaze landed on the woman standing in the middle of the Halloween tableau. It was mostly finished – only a few final touches remaining to make it perfect – but Ivy had trouble enjoying the view given the fact that the town librarian was standing in the middle of everything and she looked as if she was going to pass out. "What's going on?"

"Thank God!" Maisie barreled past Ivy and threw her arms around Jack's neck, causing him to release Ivy's hand as he caught her. Her face was red and sweating when she burrowed her face into the hollow of his neck.

Ivy pursed her lips as she studied Maisie, annoyance bubbling up as she fought to contain her temper. In addition to being one of the few full-time municipal workers in Shadow Lake, Maisie Washington was also something of a ... free spirit. In Ivy's mind that was a kind way of saying she gave more rides than an Uber driver, but now wasn't the time for petty observances. Maisie had made her interest in Jack apparent several times, which left Ivy feeling agitated even though she never considered herself a jealous person.

"What happened?" Jack asked, struggling to extricate himself from Maisie's spider-like embrace.

"It's terrible," Maisie said, her chest heaving as she dug her fingernails into the back of Jack's neck and held tighter. "I've never seen anything this terrible. I'm going to have nightmares ... which means I'm going to need someone to stick close as I sleep or I'll be too exhausted to work."

"Yes, and then how will people be able to check out books?" Ivy challenged. "We'll have a run on suicides because we won't be able to make it without your fine library leadership skills."

"Ivy." Jack's tone was low and full of warning, but Ivy ignored him.

"Hey, Maisie, I think you might get more action from Jack if you just whip your shirt completely off instead of trying to get him to look down at your cleavage that way," Ivy said. "He's going to give himself a hernia trying to dislodge you if he's not careful."

"Will you help me instead of cracking wise?" Jack challenged.

Ivy arched an eyebrow but remained where she was. "So, what happened, Maisie? Did you promise someone a roll in the cornstalks only to have them dump you in the dirt because they were afraid of crabs or something?"

"Of course not," Maisie snapped. "I was just helping put the finishing touches on this year's display when … I saw it."

"Saw what?" Jack asked, widening his eyes as he tried to use brute force to remove Maisie's hands from his neck. She was deceptively strong and he didn't want to hurt her. "Ivy, I'm not joking. Help get her off me."

"Oh, no," Ivy said, shaking her head. "You're big and strong and you're supposed to be a paragon of strength and virtue for the Shadow Lake residents. I wouldn't want to get in the way of you doing your job."

Ivy turned her attention toward the scary tableau, extending her index finger to the long picnic table in the middle of the clearing and touching the dark wood. It was coated with some sort of sticky paint to make it look as if it was splashed with blood, and whoever designed this year's scene stuffed clothing with hay and made terrifying scarecrow people for each chair. Even though the sun was bright, Ivy couldn't stop herself from shivering when she felt someone staring at her back. She turned quickly, scanning the area behind her and finding nothing but another part of the display.

"Ivy!" Jack was getting desperate and he finally grabbed Maisie around the waist and yanked her away from him. Since his arms were longer than hers, he had a distinct advantage. Maisie's face twisted when Jack placed her on the ground and took a step away from her. "Stay."

"Good doggy," Ivy absentmindedly intoned, her eyes trained on the cornstalks. She was convinced she felt someone staring at her moments before. She peered into the thick stalks, though, and didn't register even a bare hint of movement.

"No one is talking to you, Ivy," Maisie said, rolling her eyes. "I'm trying to talk to Jack."

"And I'm willing to listen as long as you keep your hands to yourself," Jack said. "My services as a police officer are open game. The rest of me is not."

Maisie jutted out her lower lip. "Ivy has sucked all of the fun out of you. You know that, right?"

"How would you know?" Ivy scoffed, her eyes moving from the stalks to the wooden crucifix at the edge of the clearing. One of the odd straw men was hanging from it, too. They'd added a weird mask to this one, though. The others had garish bags over their heads. This figure looked to have a flesh-toned mask somehow perched on the hay to make it all the more unsettling. "Jack was only in town for a month before we started dating. That's hardly enough time for you to ascertain that he's fun. I mean … I know you move fast, but even you can't move that fast."

"Hey!"

Ivy refused to turn her eyes away from the scarecrow figure even though Maisie's anger was palpable. There was something about the scarecrow that bothered her, although she couldn't immediately put her finger on it.

"Maisie, let's turn back to the problem at hand," Jack suggested. "No, you stay right there. Why were you screaming?"

"Oh, *that*," Maisie intoned, leaning forward a bit so Jack would have a clear view down the vee of her shirt. "I accidentally ran into that scarecrow over there and some of the blood fell on me. I thought it was real."

"Uh-huh." Jack worked overtime to rein in his temper. "So you screamed for no good reason?"

"I had a good reason," Maisie said. "I was afraid."

"Yeah, Jack, she needed a strong man to protect her," Ivy said, reaching over to touch the scarecrow's shoe. It was a Nike brand sneaker, which seemed like a terrible waste considering the elements would ravish it within days. The shoe was almost even with her midriff and the toe was caked with red liquid. "Her plan worked, too. We came running."

"Yes, well, I could've done without you sticking your nose into police business instead of letting Jack do his job without a chaperone," Maisie shot back. "I'm starting to think you don't trust Jack around me."

"I trust Jack just fine," Ivy said, the need to see what was under the shoe momentarily overwhelming her. "It's you I don't trust."

"Ivy, what are you doing?" Jack took a step in Ivy's direction, her fascination with the scarecrow finally catching his attention. "Do you see something?"

"Uh-huh." Ivy's heart rolled when she finally got the shoe off, this morning's breakfast threatening to make a return appearance when a human foot swam into view. "Jack … ."

"I think you know that Jack is going to get bored with you," Maisie said, refusing to give up the fight. "It's only a matter of time. Everyone knows you're weird and men don't like weird. They like me, not weird."

"I'll never get bored with her," Jack said, instinct taking over when he saw Ivy's knees begin to buckle. "Ivy!"

The last thing Ivy's mind managed to register was something stopping her body from crashing to the ground – and she had the distinct impression that it was Jack's arms, even though she couldn't see his face. Then blackness took over … along with something else.

IT WAS dark before it was light.

Ivy wasn't unconscious as much as she was in someone else's head. She couldn't explain the phenomenon. One second she was listening to Maisie hit on Jack and the next … well … the next she was somewhere else entirely.

"I don't want to die."

Ivy heard the words, but she couldn't pinpoint a location for the individual uttering them. The blackness she initially slid into was gone, but the whiteness replacing it was no better. It was light, but there was no definition to cling to.

"Hello?"

No one immediately answered, and then the voice returned. This time Ivy was certain it belonged to a man.

"I don't want to die."

That's when Ivy remembered the foot. The sight of the mounted scarecrow was so off-putting, so realistic, that she couldn't stop herself from checking closer. Her heart hammered as she unlaced the shoe and pulled. She fully expected to find nothing but straw remaining when the shoe came free. That's not what she found, though. In hindsight, she realized that the pictures of straw flitting through her head were wishful thinking. Part of her knew the tableau was real before she had confirmation.

"Who are you?" Ivy asked, swallowing hard. She felt nauseated and couldn't help but run her hand over her stomach as she tried to remain focused. She knew she wasn't in a real place and this was only happening in her head, but the urge to vomit was overwhelming and she wasn't sure she could fight it.

"I don't want to die."

The man repeated the refrain over and over. Ivy couldn't find a shadow to associate with another presence in all of the light. Instead it was just a voice saying the exact same thing over and over.

"I don't want to die."

"I can help you," Ivy called out. "I … who are you?"

"I don't want to die."

Ivy lost the battle for control of her stomach, and when she opened her mouth to ask another question, her breakfast omelet spewed out instead of words. That's when she bolted to a sitting position in the cornfield and threw up all over Jack's shoe.

"Ivy?" Jack's face was a mask of concern as he cradled her, seemingly oblivious to the fact that she'd just upchucked on his Chuck Taylors. "Honey, are you okay? Look at me."

"Oh, geez," Maisie muttered, edging closer. "What a drama queen. She just couldn't take the fact that you were more interested in me than her. Look at her face, though. She looks like a sweaty pig."

"Shut up, Maisie," Jack barked, running his hand over Ivy's forehead. "She's burning up. We have got to get her to the hospital clinic."

"Who is this 'we' you're talking about?" Maisie asked. "By the way, you have noticed that's a real human foot sticking out from that scarecrow, right?"

"I noticed," Jack replied grimly.

"Shouldn't you worry about that instead of Ivy?"

"No." Jack was grim as he balanced a confused and violently ill Ivy against his chest and leaned forward so he could dig in his pocket for his cell phone. "Hold on, honey." He punched in his partner's number and then pressed the phone to his ear. "Brian, it's Jack. I'm in the middle of the corn maze thing with Ivy. There's a body on a cross … no, a real body … and Ivy just passed out. She's throwing up and feverish. I have to get her to the clinic, but you need to get someone over here to control the scene."

Jack was silent for a moment before continuing. "I can't wait. I need to move Ivy now."

As if on cue, Ivy leaned forward and vomited again. This time she hit Maisie's expensive boots, earning a screech for her efforts.

"Omigod!"

"Come on, Ivy," Jack said, slipping his arms under her legs and hoisting her up. "I'm getting you help right now, honey. Hold on."

Four

"Max!"

Jack was focused when he emerged from the corn maze, Ivy cradled against his chest as she rested her head on his shoulder. Sweat poured from her brow and her stomach felt as if a legion of scorpions were stinging her from the inside.

Max glanced up from the blonde he was conversing with, his brow furrowed as he locked gazes with Jack. "What was the screaming about? Did someone mistake one of those straw guys as a real person? I knew that would be a bad idea."

"There's a real body in there," Jack replied, grim. "I called Brian, but I can't wait for him. Ivy is sick. I have to get her to the clinic."

Max wasn't prone to histrionic fits, although he did delve into dramatic ones when he wanted attention from time to time. His expression when he shifted his eyes to Ivy was troubled. "What's wrong with her?"

"I have no idea," Jack said. "She … touched the body and then fell over. She lost consciousness for about sixty seconds, and when she woke up she started throwing up."

"Nice." Max clearly wasn't as worried as Jack. "What did she have for breakfast?"

"The same thing I did," Jack snapped. "We got omelets at the diner. She's burning up, Max. I'm not kidding around."

Max finally sobered and closed the distance, extending his hand to press against Ivy's brow when he reached them. "You're right. How do you feel, sis?"

"I'm on fire." Ivy's voice was raspy. "I think I might be dying."

"Don't ever say that," Jack choked out, picking up his pace as he hurried past the curious onlookers. The clinic was downtown, on the other side of the police station, and it would take more time to load Ivy into his truck than it would to carry to her to the front door. "You're going to be okay."

"Maybe you should give her to me," Max suggested, falling into step with Jack. "Don't you have to stay and secure the crime scene?"

"I won't leave her," Jack said, his eyes stormy. "You wait at the maze until Brian shows up. Don't let anyone in or out."

"But … ." Max was understandably conflicted.

"That's an order," Jack barked. "Come to the clinic as soon as you can."

With those words, Jack broke into a run. He left a dumbfounded Max in his wake and he hurried toward the clinic. All he could think about was Ivy, and he was determined to make sure she came out of … whatever this was … no worse for wear.

"HER FEVER is coming down."

Jack rubbed his forehead as he paced the spot next to Ivy's bed an hour later. Max waited for Brian before heading to the clinic as instructed, but the worried man couldn't take watching his sister restlessly sleep on the bed for more than a few minutes before he excused himself to the lobby to call his parents. Jack had been alone with Ivy since then, worry plaguing him as the doctor and nurses buzzed around her prone form.

"What's wrong with her?"

"I have no idea." Dr. Martin Nesbitt graced Jack with a sympathetic look. He was well aware of the close relationship Ivy and Jack shared. He wished he had better news. "Our biggest concern was getting her fever down. If this keeps up, she should be back to normal in less than an hour."

"That's good, right?" Jack was bordering on desperate.

"That's very good," Nesbitt confirmed. "The fever was our biggest worry. It spiked high out of nowhere. You're sure she wasn't sick earlier, right?"

"She was fine," Jack replied. "She was in a good mood. She was … going on and on about the corn maze and how much she loves Halloween."

"I forgot that about her," Nesbitt said, resting the back of his hand on Ivy's forehead. "She's resting more comfortably now."

"Does that mean she's going to wake up?"

"She'll wake up."

"She's not in a coma, right?"

Nesbitt cocked an eyebrow. "Son, you need to calm down," he said. "Ivy is going to be fine. She's strong. She's always been strong."

"Then what is this?" Jack practically exploded. "She was absolutely fine until she wasn't."

"Calm down, Romeo," Max chided, striding into the room with his father on his heels. For his part, Michael Morgan looked calm but worried when he caught sight of his only daughter. "I know you and Ivy are tragically co-dependent, but I'm sure she's going to be fine."

"You can keep saying that all you want, but I'm not going to believe it until she wakes up," Jack hissed.

"Okay, you two, that will be enough of that," Michael said, holding up his hands to placate the boys. He'd started to think of them as something akin to brothers thanks to the way they interacted. He was genuinely fond of the police officer, but the last thing he needed was an explosive showdown between the two men when Ivy looked so frail. "Give me a rundown on what's happening."

Jack licked his lips and nodded as he dragged a restless hand through his hair. "We were at the corn maze and heard someone scream," he replied. "We ran in and found Maisie Washington in the middle of the maze and she was upset because she thought real blood dropped on her."

Max snorted. "She was probably just looking for attention."

"That's what I thought," Jack conceded. "I was trying to deal with Maisie while Ivy walked over to this ... scarecrow thing ... on a cross. I thought it was one of the other hay people. I think she did, too.

"For some reason, though, she jerked the shoe off the figure and it was a human foot," he continued. "The next thing I knew she dropped like a stone. She was out for about a minute and then started throwing up."

"Yes, Maisie wouldn't stop talking about Ivy ruining her boots after you left," Max intoned. "She said she was going to send a bill."

"I'll send my foot up her behind if she tries anything of the sort," Michael said, rubbing the back of his neck. "Could it be food poisoning?"

Nesbitt shook his head. "I mean, anything is possible I guess, but I'm not leaning toward that," he said.

"Jack had the exact same breakfast and food poisoning doesn't come on like that. I'm honestly not sure what it is."

"It has to be something," Jack argued. "She's healthy. She … was fighting with me two minutes before."

"I told you that would happen," Max muttered, earning a cuff from his father.

"Now is not the time, Max," Michael said. "If you're still acting like this when your mother gets here, she's not going to be nearly as pleasant as I am."

"Where is Mom?"

"She's over with your aunt at the shop," Michael replied, referring to Felicity Goodings' magic store a couple of towns over. "They're both on their way."

"Well, that should be a barrel of laughs when those two mother hens hit the room," Max said. "Ivy will have no choice but to get out of bed or they'll smother her with heaving bosoms."

"Max … stop talking," Michael warned. "Sit in that corner and zip your lips." He watched his son sheepishly sit in a chair before focusing on Jack. "I'm sorry. When he gets nervous, he babbles. It's not always pleasant babbling either."

"It's okay," Jack said. "I just … I've never seen anything like that. She frightened me."

"Well, we'll figure out what it is," Nesbitt said. "We're going to run a battery of tests on her and see if we can pinpoint a problem. I … um … ." He looked uncomfortable when he locked gazes with Jack. "Do you think there's any chance she's pregnant?"

Jack was aghast, his cheeks burning as Michael widened his eyes. "No. I … no."

"Are you sure?" Nesbitt prodded. "She's a young woman and you two are not shy about showing affection."

"We're careful," Jack muttered, steadfastly refusing to meet Michael's gaze. "She's not pregnant."

"We'll run a test to be sure," Nesbitt said. "Until then, I'm sure you have business to attend to in the corn maze. We'll keep you updated on Ivy's condition if you have to head back out there."

"I'm not leaving her." Jack's response was succinct and no-nonsense.

"It's okay, Jack," Michael said. "We'll watch her."

"No." Jack vehemently shook his head. "I left her in the hospital once before and I'll never forgive myself for doing it a second time."

"This is different," Max said. "What you did that day was … absentminded and foolish. You didn't do it because you were trying to hurt her, though. Ivy understands you have a job to do."

"No!" Jack's voice echoed in the small room. "I'm staying with her. I don't care what any of you say."

Nesbitt held up his hands in a placating manner. "Okay, son," he said. "It was just a suggestion."

"Don't make it again," Jack said, sitting in the chair next to Ivy and capturing her hand. "I'm staying right here until she opens her eyes. I want to be the first thing she sees."

"Well, that will definitely make her throw up again," Max quipped.

"Son, if you open your mouth one more time, I'm going to sew it shut," Michael warned. "The last thing we need is you making things ten times worse … if that's even possible. Do you understand?"

Max mutely nodded.

"Good," Michael intoned. "Finally something good is happening this afternoon. Max is speechless. I never thought I would see the day."

"HEY."

Ivy was confused when she opened her eyes, but the worry creasing Jack's forehead was enough to cause her stomach to quiver all over again. "Hey." Her hand shook as she lifted it to his face. He looked almost haggard. "Are you okay?"

Jack barked out a laugh as he pressed her hand to his cheek. "I think I should be asking you that, not the other way around."

"I'm not sure what happened," Ivy said, her eyes widening when she glanced around the room and found her mother, aunt, father, and brother watching her with trepidation. "Am I dying?"

"Don't ever make that joke again," Jack chided, smoothing her hair.

"I don't remember making it a first time … I mean, other than this time."

"You said it when Jack was carrying you out of the corn maze," Max offered. "He didn't take it well then either."

"I'm sorry," Ivy said, struggling to prop up her upper body on the pillows as she scanned the room. "I don't really remember that."

"It's okay," Jack said. "You were probably delirious."

"I remember throwing up on Maisie's boots," Ivy pointed out.

"Yes, but that was a fun memory," Max joked, earning a dark look from his mother. "What?"

"Ignore him." Luna Morgan was the spitting image of her daughter in most respects. She looked older than Ivy remembered, though. Apparently Ivy's brief illness took a toll on everyone she loved. "How are you, sweetie? How do you feel?"

"A little weak but otherwise okay," Ivy answered. "Can I go home now?"

Jack chuckled darkly as he rubbed her hand. "No. You can't go home until the doctor says it's okay."

"Is that going to be today?"

"I have no idea," Jack replied.

"I'll get him," Michael said, moving toward the door. "They've been running tests for hours. That's how long you've been out of it."

"The good news is that you're not pregnant," Max interjected. "That was a relief to everyone … especially Jack, because I think he was worried Dad was going to murder him if the test turned pink."

Ivy was already confused, but Max's rapid conversational offering was enough to completely muddle her head. "I'm not sure I understand," she said. "I … why would you think I'm pregnant?"

"Stop saying that word," Jack whispered, making a slashing motion across his throat when Michael cast him a dubious look as he yanked open the door. "Max isn't lying about your dad wanting to kill me."

Despite the surreal situation, Ivy couldn't help but giggle. "I guess I missed a lot, huh?"

"Don't do it again, huh?" Jack shot back, his voice cracking. "You scared the life out of me."

"I'm sorry."

"Please don't do it again," Jack said, squeezing her fingers tighter and moving his eyes to the door when Nesbitt breezed into the room. "She's awake."

"I noticed," Nesbitt said, smiling kindly at Ivy. "How are you feeling?"

"Perfect," Ivy lied. "Can I go home?"

Nesbitt acted as if he'd been expecting the question. "Not quite yet. We're still waiting on tests."

"When those come back, can I go home?" Ivy had no intention of giving up the argument.

"We'll see," Nesbitt said. "The good news is that your fever is way down and your temperature is back to normal. You haven't vomited since arriving either."

"And you're not pregnant," Max added.

"Don't make me smack you," Luna warned, wagging a finger in Max's face. "This is about your sister, not your need for attention."

"It must be Crap On Max Day," Max lamented. "I can see no other reason for this abuse."

Michael opened his mouth, a warning about a different kind of abuse on the tip of his tongue, but he snapped it shut when Brian Nixon poked his head through the doorway. His smile was friendly as he looked around the room, his weary gaze finally falling on his partner.

"I was planning on going to the maze as soon as Ivy woke up," Jack offered. "She just woke up, though. I swear."

"It's okay," Brian said. "I've been in contact with the doctor to check on her progress. We're in the process of handling the scene. The state boys have a tech team over there right now looking for evidence."

"Do you know who the guy on the cross was?" Ivy asked, her memory rushing back. "That was a real body, right?"

"It was," Brian confirmed. "It was Jeff Johnson."

Everyone exhaled heavily, the news taking the room by surprise.

"Who is that?" Jack asked.

"He's a fireman," Brian replied. "He grew up in Shadow Lake. He's well liked and a good worker."

"What happened to him?" Michael asked. "I just saw his parents at that new restaurant on the lake about two weeks ago. They were in good spirits and happy. They said Jeff was doing well, too."

"He was stabbed in the chest," Brian answered. "As for the weapon or motive, well, we're obviously still working that out. The coroner says he's been dead for about a day and it looks like he bled out from the wound. I haven't gotten any further on the investigation than that, though. I wanted to check on Ivy before collecting my partner."

Jack balked. "I can't leave her. She's sick."

"I'm not sick," Ivy countered. "I … passed out. It must've been the excitement of the day."

"Yes, that was clearly it," Jack deadpanned. "Or … not. It doesn't matter. I'm not going."

"I understand if you don't want to leave Ivy," Brian said. "I would like you with me when I start questioning people, though. Um … do you think you'll be back to work tomorrow?"

"I don't know." Jack was hesitant. He was a stickler when it came to following police procedure, and he was determined to do a good job, but he was haunted by abandoning Ivy in the hospital once before and he couldn't make himself leave her side. "I need to hear what the doctor says."

"We're still waiting on tests," Nesbitt said. "For now, she's stable and not going anywhere. You're fine to go to work for a few hours."

"No." Jack shook his head and forced a smile as he locked gazes with Ivy. "I'll stay here."

Ivy blew out a long-suffering sigh, one only a dramatic woman could muster, and tapped Jack's cheek to make sure she had his attention. "I know what's upsetting you and it's okay," she said. "My family is here. I know you need to go with Brian. I understand."

"I … ."

"Jack, as long as you come back, it's okay to go," Ivy said. "I promise I'm going to be all right."

Jack wasn't convinced, but with everyone staring at him he felt as if he didn't have a choice but to do her bidding. "I'll be back as soon as I can." He pressed a kiss to her forehead and lingered there for a moment, as if inhaling her scent. "You do everything the doctor tells you to do. I won't be far away."

"Go."

"Take care of her," Jack said, swallowing hard as he glanced at Michael. "I'm awfully fond of her."

"That makes all of us," Michael said, clapping Jack's shoulder. "We'll keep an eye on her. You have a job to do. The residents in this town need you to do it."

They were reasonable words, but Jack couldn't stop the guilt from plaguing him when he locked gazes with Ivy. "I'll be a phone call away," he said. "If you need me, call. I'll come running."

Five

"Are you okay?"

Brian slid a sidelong look toward his partner as Jack trudged up Jeff Johnson's driveway. The man looked morose. He'd assumed that was Jack's normal expression when he first came to town, but after getting together with Ivy, Brian saw more smiles than frowns. Today was obviously a different story.

"I'm fine," Jack replied, rubbing the back of his neck. "I know why we're here and what we have to do. I'm on top of it."

"That's not what I was asking, Jack," Brian said, making a clucking sound as he shook his head. "Are you okay about leaving Ivy?"

"No."

"You didn't have to come."

"Apparently I did," Jack countered. "I'm here now. Let's just do this."

Brian blew out a frustrated sigh. "You're just as dramatic as Ivy," he said. "She told you to come with me. You're not … abandoning her."

"That's not how it feels," Jack said. "I promised not to leave her again after … what I did before."

"You mean when she was shot and you freaked out because it reminded you of when you were shot?" Brian challenged. "I admit you didn't handle that well, but it was understandable given the circumstances. Ivy certainly forgave you. She's not holding a grudge."

"That doesn't mean I'm not holding one for her," Jack said. "Can we just do this? I don't want to be away from Ivy for too long. I want to hear what the doctor has to say."

"Well, at least she's not pregnant," Brian teased, earning a harsh look for his lame joke. "Oh, yeah, I heard about that. Max has a huge mouth."

"Max *does* have a huge mouth," Jack agreed. "I'm glad he's with Ivy, though. He'll … take care of her."

"Ivy has been taking care of herself for a very long time," Brian pointed out. "It's great that you two are gooey and in love, but … she's going to be okay. She might've just gotten lightheaded or something. It happens."

"No, not like this it doesn't," Jack said. "She went rigid just as it happened – as if she was seeing something – and then she fell. Being lightheaded doesn't explain her throwing up the way she did either."

"Maybe her stomach flipped when she fell," Brian said. "You don't know something is wrong until the doctor tells you something is wrong. Try looking on the bright side of things."

"I've been looking on the bright side of things since I found her," Jack said. "That's exactly why I don't want to lose her."

"You're not going to lose her," Brian scoffed. "It's a small medical ailment. It will probably end up being something you guys laugh about years from now. You'll tell Ivy she fainted because your mere presence overwhelmed her. She'll pick a fight and say it was your smell or something."

"That would actually be nice," Jack said.

"Everything will be fine," Brian said. "You'll see."

Jack wanted to believe him, but he couldn't until he heard it from an actual doctor.

KAREN JOHNSON looked confused when she opened the door, her hand instinctively going to her protruding belly as she rubbed it. Brian knew she was pregnant, but he forgot in all of the excitement over discovering her husband's body. This was going to make things worse.

"Is something going on?" Karen knit her eyebrows together. "I … has something happened?"

"Hey, Karen," Brian said, his tone kind as he tried to remain strong. This was his least favorite part of the job. "Can we come inside?"

As if sensing her world was about to change, Karen gripped the open door and shook her head. "No, just tell me what's going on. I … tell me."

Brian couldn't help but wonder if she irrationally believed she could change her future by not granting them entry to the house. He'd seen stranger things happen. Of course, since she was pregnant, the house might not be up to her typically lofty cleanliness standards either. Women were funny that way.

"There's been an … incident," Brian said, wetting his lips. "I think maybe you should sit down."

"I don't want to sit down," Karen gritted out, terror flitting across her pleasing features. Only moments before she exuded that "glow" only pregnant women can boast. Now she looked pale and ghastly. "What's happened? Was there a fire? Was Jeff hurt in a fire?"

"When was the last time you saw Jeff?" Jack asked, adopting a gentle tone.

"He's been at the station for the past two days," Karen replied, annoyed. "Once the baby comes he's going to be taking some time off so he's making it up to his coworkers now and taking extra shifts. It's kind of annoying because I'm terrified I'm going to go into labor when he's not around, but it will be better once the baby comes."

"I actually think I heard that at the diner the other day," Brian said, wanting to kick himself for the way the notification was going. "Karen, um, we have something to tell you and it's not good news. I really think you need to sit down."

"I don't want to sit down!" Karen's face was completely white and tears threatened to spill over onto her cheeks. "Where is Jeff? Is he okay? Is he in the hospital?"

Brian opted to rip the bandage off in one clean motion. He had to tell her, and he couldn't keep pussyfooting around. Shadow Lake was small, so the man didn't have to deliver bad news like this very often. It still had to be done on rare occasions, though, and Karen was suffering because of his slow approach.

"We found Jeff's body in the corn maze this morning," Brian said. "He's dead. The coroner believes he's been dead for at least twenty-four hours. I'm so sorry, Karen. I … ."

Brian didn't get a chance to finish because Karen's wail drowned out the rest of his words. It was just empty sentiment, he reminded himself. He could offer the woman nothing by way of solace.

Karen teetered against the wall, her balance slipping until Jack stepped forward and steadied her. He looked as stricken as the new widow, and Brian realized too late that the interaction would have a profound effect on his partner as well. This was the last thing Jack wanted to see when he was freaking out about Ivy.

"Karen, we need to get you inside," Brian said gently. "Come on. We'll help you call people and get settled. It's … ." Brian was going to say it would be all right. He knew that wasn't the truth, though. "We'll get your family over here to help you right away."

"HEY, honey."

Sitting through Karen's meltdown was pure torture for Jack. Sure, it was part of the job and he knew it came with the territory, but watching a woman realize the life she planned was never going to happen taxed Jack's already frayed nerves. Brian recognized that his partner needed to get back to Ivy and didn't put up a fight when Jack announced he was returning to the clinic. In truth, they couldn't do anything until the tech team started feeding them information. Questioning the other firefighters and corn maze workers could wait until the following day.

"Hi." Ivy looked markedly better when she locked gazes with Jack. "I wasn't expecting you so soon."

"Yes, well, I think I'm addicted to your face," Jack said, sitting in the chair next to her bed and smiling. "I couldn't stay away for one second longer. It literally would've killed me."

Misuse of the word "literally" was one of Ivy's pet peeves. "It literally would not have killed you," she argued.

"Well, it felt as if I was dying," Jack said, stroking her soft cheek with his thumb. Her temperature was back to normal and the only thing out of the ordinary was the dark circles under her eyes. "How are you feeling?"

"I feel fine, Jack," Ivy replied. "If you're going to hover, you can do it in the lobby with the rest of my family."

"Yes, I saw them out there when I came in," Jack said. "Max said you banished them. How come?"

"Because I don't need people smothering me with good intentions and worry," Ivy answered. "It makes me agitated."

"I think you just like being bossy."

"I think you're going to have to join them if you're not careful," Ivy warned, her expression serious. "I mean it."

"I like it when you use your stern face," Jack said, taking Ivy by surprise when he stood and slipped his arm under her legs to slide her body over and make room so he could join her on the bed. Ivy opened her mouth to argue but ultimately opted for another course of action when she saw the lines around Jack's eyes. He looked exhausted. Instead, she rested her cheek on his chest and let him hold her. "Thank you." Jack's voice was barely a murmur as he ran his hand over the back of her head.

"For what?" Ivy asked, genuinely curious.

"For being sweet enough to know I'll have some sort of freakout if you try separating yourself from me right now," Jack replied, guileless. "I can't take it and you recognized that, so instead of fighting you gave in. That rarely happens, but when it does, it's magical."

Ivy snorted as she rested her hand on Jack's chest, taking solace in the steady beat of his heart. "I really am okay."

"You didn't see things from my perspective," Jack countered. "You dropped so fast, honey. I … still don't understand what happened."

Instead of immediately responding, Ivy leaned forward so she could peer into the hallway and then glanced around the hospital room in a conspiratorial manner. It was almost as if she was a spy and trying to impart vital government secrets on him without anyone being the wiser.

"I think I know what happened," Ivy said finally, causing Jack's eyebrows to fly into his hairline. "You're not going to like it, though."

"You're not pregnant, right?" Jack had no idea why he went for the joke, but for some reason it lightened the mood and caused Ivy to giggle.

"No, and I would've paid money to see your face when that happened in front of my father," Ivy said. "You don't have to worry about that. I'm very diligent with my pills."

"I'm not worried about that," Jack said. "If it happens, it happens."

Ivy's mouth dropped open. "What?"

"You heard me," Jack said. "I'm not taking it back. Unfortunately, though, that is not the focus of this conversation. We'll fight about that when you're back on your feet and I have no reason to worry."

"You don't have a reason to worry now," Ivy said. "At least … not anything in the medical realm, which is what you seem to be obsessing about."

Jack was legitimately curious as he tipped up her chin so he could study her beautiful face. "What do you mean?"

"I saw something, Jack." Ivy wet her lips, her eyes conflicted. She was clearly worried about telling Jack what really happened at the corn maze.

Jack rubbed the back of her neck. "Okay. Tell me what you saw."

"You're being really calm, but you're going to hate what I'm about to tell you."

"Well, you can't be sure of that until you tell me," Jack argued. "So … tell me."

"It was like I couldn't stop myself," Ivy said, her voice quavering. "I knew before I knew. Does that make sense?"

"You knew what?"

"That the scarecrow was really a body," Ivy replied. "I … felt it. Or maybe my mind recognized something was really wrong and that's why I couldn't stop myself from taking off the shoe."

"Yes, we're going to have to make sure the state police have a copy of your fingerprints on file to rule them out, by the way," Jack said.

"They're on record."

Jack pursed his lips, surprised. "Your fingerprints are on record? Why?"

"I might've been arrested a time or two for drinking in a field when I was a teenager," Ivy replied. "It was nothing serious. Chill."

"Ah, the joys of living in a small town," Jack said, chuckling. "In the city, the cops come after you for drinking in vacant lots and everyone bolts before tickets are issued."

"Yes, well, everyone knows everyone in Shadow Lake," Ivy said. "That's not really part of the story."

"Oh, right," Jack said, smiling. He found himself relaxing the more she talked. She really did sound like her normal self. "Go on. I'm listening."

"The second I pulled the shoe off and realized it was a body … um … I went to another place."

Ivy's eyes were full of fear – which Jack hated – but he wasn't entirely sure what she was trying to explain to him.

"Honey, you didn't go anywhere," Jack said. "I caught you before you hit the ground. You were with me the entire time."

"I know my body didn't go anywhere," Ivy said. "I just … my head did."

"Oh." Jack's forehead creased as he rubbed her cheek. "Where did you go?"

"I don't know," Ivy replied, studying Jack's face for signs he was going to bolt. This was too weird for any normal man to put up with. "It was black at first … and then white. I kept hearing someone say that they didn't want to die and my body hurt and my stomach was on fire."

"You kept hearing someone say they didn't want to die?" Jack was intrigued.

"Yes."

"Was it a man or a woman?"

"Man."

"Do you think it was Jeff Johnson?" Jack asked. "Do you think you were hearing his last thoughts or something?"

Ivy was dumbfounded. "That's all you're going to say? Aren't you freaked out? Don't you think I'm crazy or something?"

"No." Jack's answer was simple, and he almost enjoyed the flustered look on her face. In truth, her explanation made him feel markedly better because it explained her illness in a manner that didn't require serious medical care.

"Why not?" Ivy almost looked disappointed by Jack's lack of reaction.

"Because this isn't the first time you've proven that you're special," Jack answered. "I mean that in more ways than one, by the way. I don't think it's a big deal. You're magical, Ivy. If you managed to get into Jeff's head and hear his last thoughts, well, you might be able to help us track down his killer once you get settled and have a chance to think over things.

"Now, I'm not happy your brain was overloaded and you got sick, but this admission is so much better than you having a physical ailment that could make you weak or eventually take you from me," he continued. "I'm … relieved. I'm also in awe because you're amazing."

Ivy pressed the heel of her hand to her forehead. "I thought you would freak out."

"Well, then you need to get to know me better."

"I'm not sure that's possible," Ivy muttered, her blue eyes latching onto his serious brown orbs. "Are you really okay with this?"

"I'm really okay with you and so thankful you're all right," Jack replied. "We'll figure it out. I don't want you worrying or anything. This is just a new … wrinkle."

"It's more than a wrinkle," Ivy argued. "I threw up on your shoes."

"Yes, and that was gross," Jack said. "I would gladly buy a new pair of shoes every day for the rest of my life if it means you're around to throw up on them, though."

Ivy's expression softened. "That's somehow romantic and gross at the same time."

"I do my best."

Ivy wrapped her arms around Jack's waist and burrowed her face in the hollow of his neck. "Thank you for not freaking out."

"Thank you for being you," Jack murmured, kissing the top of her head. "We'll figure this out. I promise."

"I hope so." Ivy and Jack lapsed into comfortable silence for several minutes. Ivy was the first to break the mood. "So … can I go home?"

Jack chuckled, delighted and happy. "I will talk to the doctor and see what he says. No promises."

"I don't want to stay in the hospital alone."

"You won't be alone," Jack said. "If you're staying here, I will be here with you. If you're going home, I'm the one who is going to dote on you there."

"I guess I can live with that."

"Good." Jack pressed a solid kiss to her forehead. "As long as you're alive, I can live with anything."

Six

"I can't believe you cooked breakfast."

Ivy stared at her plate, which was heaping with eggs and hash browns, and shook her head. Jack had been nothing but attentive since Dr. Nesbitt cleared her to go home the previous evening. He'd doted on her, tucked her in, and even gotten out of bed to cover her feet … twice. As cute as she found his ministrations, Ivy was starting to chafe.

"Just because I generally let you cook breakfast, that doesn't mean I'm an oaf in the kitchen," Jack said, pushing a glass of juice in Ivy's direction. "Do you have everything you need?"

Ivy ran her tongue over her teeth as she silently reminded herself that Jack didn't mean to be such a mother hen. He simply couldn't help himself and she should take it as a compliment. "I'm good."

"Great." Jack sat in the chair across from her and prepared to dig into his own breakfast. "Have you talked to your dad? Is he going to run the nursery today?"

Ivy owned a plant and tree nursery, which was located on the other side of her property. It was a simple five-minute walk through the trees between her house and the business she started from scratch. Even though the season was winding down, the nursery garnered solid business until the end of November. During the winter months, Ivy worked on manufacturing the lotions, body sprays, and soaps she sold as part of a side business.

"He is," Ivy confirmed, tugging on her limited patience. "That's not a new thing, though. He was always going to run the nursery today because I'm supposed to help with the festival preparations at the greenhouse and downtown."

Jack balked. "That was before, though. You need a day to recuperate."

"I'm fine, Jack."

"You're not fine. You passed out and threw up all over everything."

"Yes, and that's exactly what I wanted to be reminded of as I'm trying to eat breakfast," Ivy deadpanned, her eyes flashing. "I feel fine. I feel refreshed, even. I slept like a rock."

"I know," Jack said, his expression unreadable. "You snored so loudly I thought you would wake the dead."

"I don't snore!"

"You did last night," Jack shot back, the corners of his mouth twitching. "I thought it was cute. I actually liked it because the noise made it so I didn't have to wake up every five minutes to make sure you were still breathing."

"You wouldn't have done that."

"Don't sell yourself short," Jack said. "I'm extremely fond of you." He wanted to say something else, but since he sensed an argument brewing, he didn't want to taint the big moment with a big fight. The longer he waited to make the declaration, though, the harder it was to find the words.

"I'm extremely fond of you, too," Ivy said, her eyes softening. "I'm sorry I snapped at you. That wasn't fair."

"I'm used to it."

"It still wasn't fair."

"I actually enjoyed it because that means you're feeling fiery," Jack said. "I like that you're feeling fiery. That makes it apparent that you're well on your way to recovery."

"I'm already recovered."

"After another day of rest you'll be recovered," Jack corrected. "For now you're homebound. You're going to settle on the couch with a pot of tea, a blanket, and that obnoxious cat that keeps trying to smother me in my sleep. That way I won't have to worry about you."

"Oh, that does sound like a nice day," Ivy said, her voice positively dripping with fake sincerity. "That's not what's going to happen, though."

Despite his best efforts to the contrary, Jack found his temper flaring. "Ivy, you were in the hospital yesterday."

"And I'm fine today," Ivy said. "I'm going to help with the festival decorations. I promised."

"I'm sure whoever is organizing the event will understand," Jack argued. "All you have to do is place a call. You can help setting up tomorrow."

"I'm going today." Ivy was done messing around. "I feel fine. I feel great even. I want to help with the festival. It's my favorite event of the entire year."

Jack felt his resolve waning due to the earnest expression on her face. He didn't want to cause her a moment of unhappiness, but he also wanted her safe. "I'm not sure I'll be able to live with that," he said. "I have a lot of work to do on Jeff Johnson's death today because I slacked off yesterday. I ... won't be able to check in on you."

Ivy made an exaggerated face that would've been comical under different circumstances. "I don't need you to check in on me."

"Yes, well, I can't help but feel as if it's my duty."

"Well, pick another duty," Ivy suggested. She was ramping up for a big fight and she didn't care if she hurt his feelings in the process. He needed to get a grip. "I'm going."

"Not if I tie you to the bed you're not."

"Oh, that sounds like a fun game for later."

Jack didn't want to smile, but he couldn't help himself. "You're such a pain in the … ."

"Jack, look at it from another direction," Ivy suggested, opting to change tactics. "If I'm stuck alone out here all day, there will be no one to help if I have another fit. I love Nicodemus dearly, but he can't operate the phone. He doesn't have opposable thumbs and only speaks to me."

As if sensing Ivy was talking about him, the black cat rubbed himself against her legs under the table.

"I … didn't think of that," Jack admitted, rubbing his finger over the tender spot between his eyebrows. "I'll call Max and see if he can spend the day with you."

"Max is going to be down at the festival," Ivy said. "He likes hitting on the haystack honeys and they're all going to be there. I'll actually be better off at the festival because it will be filled with people – and right across the road from the hospital."

Jack was caught. Her argument held a lot of merit. He also knew she was leaving out a large portion of her plans from the retelling. "If I agree to this, I expect you to keep your nose out of the investigation," he said. "This is a police matter and you're not an officer."

Ivy narrowed her eyes. "I'm the one who found his body."

"That's the only way I'll agree to this," Jack said. "If you don't promise to stay out of the investigation, you're staying here."

Ivy was affronted. "You can't force me to stay here. You're not my boss."

"No, but I am the man who … adores you," Jack said. "If I have to call your mother to make sure you do the right thing, I'll do it. I don't care how angry you get."

Ivy's mouth dropped open as the potential horror washed over her. "You would turn my own mother on me? Are you a monster?"

This time Jack's smile was wide and heartfelt. "I would do anything to keep you well and safe."

Ivy blew out a frustrated sigh. "Fine. I won't stick my nose into the investigation. Are you happy?"

"I'm *happier*," Jack clarified. "I won't be happy until we solve this and I can enjoy the Halloween festival with you. We'll take all of that one step at a time, though."

"HOW IS Ivy?"

Brian met Jack in front of the police station shortly before nine. He was happy to see Jack's color back, and the man didn't look nearly as dour as he did the previous day.

"She's good," Jack replied. "She's at the festival working."

Brian pursed his lips and glanced over his shoulder, the urge to smirk overwhelming when he saw Ivy in the thick of things as she and Max worked on decorating a table. They seemed animated as they talked to one another, and Ivy truly didn't look as if she'd undergone any sort of ordeal. "She looks good."

"She looks beautiful," Jack corrected. "She's still a pain."

Brian snorted, relieved that his partner was back to his usual self. "You like it when she's a pain," he said. "Admit it."

"I don't like it at all," Jack argued. "I think she should be a demure woman and do what she's told."

Brian knew that wasn't even remotely the truth. Jack and Ivy enjoyed the fight as much as they did making up. "Ah, I'm taking it you put your foot down and told her to stay home and she explained to you that wasn't going to happen."

"Pretty much," Jack confirmed. "She said she was an adult and that she can do whatever she wants to do. Then she pointed out that being home alone wasn't necessarily safe if she passed out again, and at least here she would have people surrounding her and easy access to the clinic if it happened in the town square."

"Oh, so she used logic," Brian teased. "That must've killed you."

"You have no idea," Jack said. "We came to an agreement, though. As long as she sticks to the festival and doesn't get involved with the investigation, things are going to be fine. She understands that Jeff Johnson's death has nothing to do with her and she promised to keep out of trouble."

Brian guffawed loudly enough he caused Jack to jolt. "Oh, boy, you're so funny," he said. "You know darned well she won't be able to keep her nose out of this. That's not in her wheelhouse."

"I know," Jack said, heaving out a sigh. "If she can put up a decent effort to stay out of it for one day, though,

I'll take that as a win. I need to know she's completely better before she goes off the rails."

"Well, at least you have reasonable expectations," Brian said. "We need to focus on work, though."

"Right," Jack said, shaking himself out of his reverie. "Where are we heading first?"

"The firehouse."

"That seems like as good a place as any to start."

"I STILL can't believe it."

Brad Gardner was chief of Shadow Lake's volunteer fire department and he met Jack and Brian at the door when they approached the station. He seemed to be expecting them.

"I think everyone is having trouble wrapping their heads around it," Brian acknowledged. "Jeff was a good guy and this was … an unpleasant way to go."

"Someone said he was stabbed in the chest," Brad prodded. "Is that true?"

"We really can't go into those details while the investigation is active," Brian said.

"I understand," Brad said. "It's just … so surreal."

"Yeah, well, we'll catch whoever did this and hopefully things will be surreal for him when he's behind bars, too," Brian said. "What we're trying to do right now is get a feeling for Jeff's movement over the course of the forty-eight hours before his death."

"Okay," Brad said. "How can I help?"

"When we made notification with Karen yesterday, she said Jeff was staying at the firehouse for several nights because he was trying to get ahead before the baby was born," Brian replied. "I'm guessing since you guys are a volunteer department, that means you trade off shifts."

"Pretty much," Brad confirmed. "We honestly don't have a lot of fires, as you know. We get some during dry conditions in the summer – and the Fourth of July is always a busy time thanks to that boneheaded fireworks law – but other than that we only go out on runs every few weeks. You guys take the other calls."

"Still, you staff the firehouse twenty-four hours a day, right?" Jack asked.

Brad nodded. "We do," he said. "We maintain due diligence on that. We have enough volunteers so no one has to do more than a night a week, though, and it's more often like a night every two weeks because I take half the nights."

"How come?" Jack was legitimately curious.

"Because I'm the only one who gets paid and that seems unfair to the other guys," Brad replied. "I make sure to check in at least once a day. This is only a part-time job for me, but I take it seriously."

"No one is accusing you of anything, Brad," Brian chided. "What can you tell me about Jeff's recent shifts, though?"

"Um … well … that's just it." Brad shifted from one foot to the other and averted his eyes from Brian's steady gaze. "You said that Jeff died twenty-four hours before his body was found and he was supposed to be at the station, right?"

"Probably," Brian replied. "We're still pinning down an exact time of death, but that's what the coroner gave us to work with."

"Well, if that's the case, then … ." Brad rolled his neck until it cracked, discomfort practically wafting off of him.

"Just tell us, Brad," Brian urged. "We're going to find out eventually."

"Jeff wasn't here that night," Brad said. "I was monitoring the station that night and I never saw him."

"But Karen said that he was at the station banking time," Jack said. "Why would she think that?"

"Um … I don't want to speak ill of the dead."

"We need all of the information," Brian said. "Tell us."

"I'm not big on idle gossip, but if you listen to some of the talk and believe it, Jeff was seeing someone on the side," Brad said, holding up his hands as if to ward off an unpleasant argument. "I've never seen it myself, but that was the rumor."

"His wife is very pregnant," Jack said, disgust rolling through his stomach. "You heard he was seeing someone else when she's about to give birth?"

"I'm just telling you what I heard," Brad said. "I don't have proof and I never cared enough about the situation to get proof. I didn't think it mattered … until now."

"Yeah, well it definitely matters now," Brian intoned, exchanging a wary look with Jack. "I don't suppose you know who this supposed side action was with, do you?"

Brad shook his head. "I have no idea … and I'm horrified to even say anything given the ordeal Karen is going through. If this gets out … ."

"We'll do what we can," Brian said, clapping Brad's shoulder. "I can't make any promises in case the death is somehow related to the affair, but if it's not, we'll do our best to keep it quiet."

"That's all I ask," Brad said. "Is there anything else?"

"I guess not," Brian replied, scratching his cheek. "Can you think of anyone who would know who this woman is?"

"I would just ask some of the other volunteers," Brad answered. "I honestly have no idea."

"Thanks for your time."

Seven

"I think this will look nice for the lotions and stuff," Ivy said, her hands on her hips as she stared at her freshly-decorated table. "What do you think?"

"That you're a pain when it comes to Halloween," Max replied, not missing a beat.

When Ivy slid her gaze in his direction, she found him staring at a well-endowed blonde standing close to one of the game stations. He wasn't even paying attention to her table. "You are a pig." Ivy flicked Max's ear, causing him to yelp. "Leave that poor girl alone. She's like half your age."

"She is not fifteen," Max replied dryly, rubbing his injured ear. "That was mean, by the way. I've been helping you for an hour straight and what's my payment? You're a terrible sister."

Ivy made a disgusted face. "I am the best sister in the world and you're lucky to have me," she shot back. "You should be thankful to have a sister like me … and that girl is barely legal, so you need to stop looking at her."

"Yes, but she's legal," Max said, his grin wolfish. "Come on. Don't you think we would make a striking couple?"

"You just like her boobs," Ivy replied, tamping down her irritation. In truth, she knew Max would never touch the girl and he was only flirting because he enjoyed the endeavor. In actuality, he often treated it like a sport. "I've got twenty bucks that says that's all padding."

"I might take you up on that bet just so I can find out," Max teased, poking her side. He studied her for a moment, his expression shifting from mirthful to sober. "How are you feeling?"

"I'm fine, Max," Ivy said, her voice tinged with agitation. "I wish everyone would stop hovering."

"We hover because we love you."

"That doesn't make it easier to swallow."

"You'll live," Max said. "Speaking of living, though, how is Jack?"

"Jack is fine," Ivy replied. "How does Jack's well-being have anything to do with living, though?"

"Because he was not amused when you announced you were dying yesterday," Max said. "For the record, I wasn't amused either. That was pretty scary."

"I didn't mean to upset everyone," Ivy said, adjusting her attitude. Life would be worse if no one cared about her, she reminded herself. Her close circle of friends and family was small, but she wouldn't trade them for anything. "I'm still not sure what happened. I think I just got overexcited."

"I don't believe that for a second, but if you want to keep telling that story, you're going to need to muster some more conviction," Max said. "No one is going to believe your version of events if you put so little effort into it."

Ivy chewed on her lip, momentarily debating whether she could impart the truth on her brother without freaking him out. She was almost relieved when two figures closed in on them and took the decision out of her hands.

"Ivy!"

Ivy's eyes widened when she caught sight of a familiar teenager, giggling when the rambunctious girl threw her arms around Ivy's neck and pulled her in for a tight hug.

"Hello, Jessica. How are you?"

"I'm good." The girl's eyes sparkled as she looked Ivy over. It had been weeks since they'd seen each other. Jessica was still fragile after being held captive for several years and slipping into her old life wasn't seamless. That didn't mean she wasn't giving it her best effort. "I haven't seen you in forever."

"That's because you've been busy," Ivy said, smiling kindly at the small boy hiding behind Jessica's legs. Noah looked happy and healthy despite being ripped from the only home he ever knew. Jessica gave birth to him during her captivity and thought he was dead. Instead, her kidnapper's wife raised the boy as her own. Now Jessica and her parents were making a life with Noah … and it was a work in progress. "How are you, Noah?"

The boy didn't answer, instead sticking his thumb in his mouth and shaking his head. He was unbelievably shy, but Ivy was hopeful he would overcome that when he felt more settled. She took a calm approach when dealing with him. Max was another story.

"How are you doing, sport?" Max grabbed Noah around the waist and swung him off the ground, smiling when the boy wildly giggled. "Oh, what's that noise? Did I hear a laugh?"

Noah giggled again, causing Ivy's heart to warm. She wasn't sure Jessica or Noah would be able to overcome the difficulties life threw at them. She was happy to be mistaken, because they were both thriving.

"What are you doing here?" Ivy asked, turning her attention to Jessica. She lived one town over and only visited on rare occasions – usually opting to head straight for Ivy's house rather than risk people in town trying to talk to her – so her appearance in the busy town square was surprising.

"I heard that Shadow Lake does Halloween right," Jessica replied. "I'm not sure I can come over here and be around a bunch of people after dark … I'm not ready for that yet … but I thought Noah might want to see all of the decorations. He had an appointment with Dr. Nesbitt today so it wasn't out of our way or anything."

"Is everything okay?"

"He's fine," Jessica answered, smiling at the small boy as Max put him on his shoulders and made monkey noises as he hopped around. "I just wanted to make sure."

"That's a relief," Ivy said. "How are things going with your parents?"

"Good. It's all … really good. They adore Noah and they make sure to help so I'm not overwhelmed. I don't know what I would do without them."

"Well, you don't have to contemplate that for a long time," Ivy said. "You might not have picked the right time to visit Shadow Lake, though. You heard we found a body in the corn maze, right?"

"I did hear that on the radio," Jessica confirmed. "I can guarantee we won't be going to the corn maze. Right now we're just watching everyone set up and having a few treats."

"Treats?" Max made an exaggerated face. "I love treats!"

"Candy!" Noah excitedly waved his arms.

"We have candy at the nursery if you want to head out there," Ivy offered. "We're about done here and I have to start on the greenhouse next."

"What's wrong with the greenhouse?"

"Oh, nothing. I just decorate it and set it up as a haunted attraction every year. That's my next task."

"Oh, that sounds fun," Jessica said. "Do you mind if we stop out there? I mean, we don't want to get in your way or anything."

"You're never in the way," Ivy said. "My dad is out there and Max is coming to help. It will be fun."

Max groaned. "I didn't say I would help. You're just trying to lure me away from the honeys."

"I'm trying to save you from yourself," Ivy corrected.

"Fine." Max wrinkled his nose as he glanced at Noah. "Do you want me to fill you full of sugar?"

Noah smiled brightly. "Candy?"

"Candy."

"Candy!"

The little boy's enthusiasm was so infectious Ivy couldn't help but giggle. "Candy it is."

HELLO! It's my favorite child."

Michael swooped in twenty minutes later and removed Noah from Max's arms before his son could put up a fight, ignoring the customers milling around Ivy's nursery as he focused on something more important – and ten times more adorable.

"Thanks, Dad," Max said dryly, shaking his head. "It's good to feel loved."

"And here I thought he was talking about me," Ivy teased, grinning.

"You're my favorite child some of the time," Michael said, making a face to entertain Noah. "You don't let me carry you around anymore, though."

"No, that's Jack's job," Max said, winking.

"How is Jack?" Jessica smiled at the mention of the police officer. In the days following her escape, she was terrified of Jack because of his size. Now she knew him well enough to realize he was nothing more than an overgrown teddy bear. "I haven't seen him the last few times I've stopped over."

"He's good," Ivy replied. "He's working on the Jeff Johnson case. He was the dead man in the corn maze."

"Did you know him?"

"We all knew him," Max said. "He was a good guy … although … ."

Ivy ran her tongue over her teeth and narrowed her eyes. "Although what?"

"It's nothing," Max said hurriedly. "I just heard a few whispers about Jeff over the past week or so. It's weird because I didn't remember the gossip until right now. I didn't even think about it when the body was found yesterday. Of course, I didn't see it and had no idea who it belonged to when Jack started yelling about getting you to the hospital."

"Hospital?" Jessica was beyond confused. "Why did you go to the hospital, Ivy?"

"It's nothing," Ivy said, waving off Jessica's concern as she scorched Max with a death glare. "Max is … overreacting."

"Yes, Max is a regular soap opera siren when he feels like being dramatic," Michael said, tipping Noah upside down and pretending to munch on the boy's feet as the toddler giggled hysterically. "He's not being dramatic this time, though. Ivy passed out at the corn maze after discovering the body … and then got violently ill. She had to be checked out at the hospital, and I'm pretty sure she's supposed to be resting instead of running around."

"Oh, now you're happy to be my dad," Ivy deadpanned, rolling her eyes. "When it comes time to boss me around, then I'm your favorite child."

"Nope. Noah is still my favorite child today. Isn't that right, Noah?"

"Candy!"

"Candy? I think I can hook you up," Michael said, flipping Noah around and placing him on the ground. "Ivy happens to have an entire box full of candy in the greenhouse. I'm sure I can get you into a sugar coma before your mom takes you home."

Noah glanced at Jessica, unsure. He was still getting used to a new "mom."

"It's okay," Jessica said, smiling. "I'll be right here when you get back."

"Don't give him so much candy he throws up," Ivy called to her father's back. "If you do that, you'll be the one picking it up."

"Since you threw up on Maisie's boots yesterday, that's not much of a threat," Max pointed out. "You didn't have to clean up your mess."

"Shut up, Max." Ivy cuffed her brother as Jessica snickered. "It really wasn't anything serious. I got lightheaded and passed out. I'm perfectly fine today."

"You got lightheaded?" Jessica tugged on a strand of her hair and glanced around to make sure no one was eavesdropping before lowering her voice. "You're not pregnant, are you?"

Ivy was mortified. "No!"

"I thought the same thing," Max said. "I was looking forward to a niece or nephew. Alas, the doctor says that's not the case. I think Dad was upset at the possibility at first, but seeing him with Noah makes me realize he'll warm to the reality when it happens."

Ivy slapped her hand over her eyes. "I cannot believe you just brought that up again. It's so … ridiculous. Jack and I are nowhere near ready to have kids."

"I think Jack will make a wonderful father," Jessica enthused.

Ivy thought the same thing. That didn't mean she was ready to test the theory. "Well, when that day comes, I'll make sure the two of you are the first to know," Ivy said, desperately searching her mind for something to distract the giggling twosome. Then she remembered Max's words from earlier. "What did you mean when you said you heard gossip about Jeff?"

"Oh, *that*," Max said, rolling his neck. "I should've known you wouldn't forget that."

"No, I have no intention of forgetting that," Ivy said. "Talk."

"It's just … you know I hang out with some of the volunteer firefighters down at the bar, right?"

Ivy nodded. She'd often thought Max would be a good fit for the department … if he ever wanted to cut down on his social schedule, that is. "Yeah."

"Well, they let slip the other night – I guess it would've been Tuesday – that there's a rumor making the rounds about Jeff cheating on Karen."

Ivy was appalled. "She's like ten months pregnant!"

"I know," Max said, bobbing his head. "That's why the gossip is so good."

"It's not good," Ivy countered, her voice going shrill. "That's terrible. Karen is carrying Jeff's child. You're basically saying that now she has to get over his death and put up with the fact that he was cheating on her, all the while she's getting ready to push a human being out of her loins. Is that what you're saying?"

"I would never use the word loins," Max said dryly. "The rest sounds about right, though."

"That is horrible," Ivy said, rubbing her cheek as Jessica made sympathetic clucking noises. "I mean … who would sleep with a man knowing that his wife is going to give birth to his child any moment? That would have to be a special kind of … ."

"Slut?" Max supplied.

"I was going to say terrible person, but slut works, too," Ivy said. "Do you know who he was supposedly running around with?"

"I do," Max confirmed, pressing his lips together.

"Do you want to tell me?"

"No."

"Max!"

"Fine." Max made an exaggerated face as he squared his shoulders. "It was Maisie Washington."

Ivy's heart sank at the news, disgust filling her stomach and turning it into a pit of hard bile. "Maisie? You've got to be kidding me. She was the one who started screaming by the body."

"I … huh. I never considered that," Max said. "Maybe she killed him."

"Or maybe she knows who killed him," Ivy suggested, her mind working overtime. "I need to call Jack. He should hear about this because it changes things in the investigation."

"I think that's a great idea," Max said, glancing over his sister's shoulder and frowning. "You should totally do that ... just as soon as you deal with this customer."

Ivy was confused. "What customer?"

"That one," Max said, pointing. "She looks angry."

"Oh, hey, isn't that the woman you were just talking about?" Jessica lifted her chin. "She's the woman from the dance, right?"

Ivy's heart sank when she realized Jessica was right and Maisie was storming in their direction. She didn't look particularly happy. In fact, she looked outraged and ready for a fight. "Batten down the hatches," she said. "Something tells me this ride is about to get bumpy."

"Something tells me you're right," Max intoned. "Bye!"

Eight

"Don't even think about it."

Ivy snagged Max's arm before he could make his getaway, jerking him back so she could keep him close as Maisie closed the distance. She looked livid. Generally that wouldn't be cause for concern, but Max's gossipy tidbit – coupled with Maisie's sudden arrival – made Ivy understandably nervous.

"If you need me to punch her when she's not looking, I'm totally game," Jessica offered, the set of her jaw grim.

Ivy fought the mad urge to laugh at the teenager's serious expression. "I think we're going to be okay," she said. "If she does attack, I'll handle it. I'm an expert at pulling hair."

"Tell me about it," Max grumbled. "I still remember the time you yanked that huge chunk of hair out of my head because I hid in the shower and jumped out when you were brushing your teeth that one time."

"You had that coming."

"I'm not denying that," Max said. "Something tells me Maisie is going to have it coming before the end of the day, too."

"Something tells me you're right," Ivy muttered, plastering a fake smile on her face for Maisie's benefit when she stopped in front of the small group. Maisie's chest heaved and her eyes flashed as she glanced from face to face. "Welcome to the nursery," Ivy said automatically. "Can I show you something in a nice fall mum?"

"Oh, that was hilarious," Max said, smirking.

Maisie ignored Max and gave Jessica a cursory glance before focusing on Ivy. "You."

"Me?"

"You."

"I think she's trying to tell you something, Ivy," Max said. "I think she's saying … you."

"Shut up," Maisie snapped, her nostrils flaring as she stared down Max. "No one is talking to you. Why are you even here? Don't you have a job or something?"

"I could say the same thing about you," Max shot back, not missing a beat. "Isn't your street corner lonely without you peddling your wares?"

"Max." Ivy pressed her lips together and offered her brother a small headshake. She would usually enjoy any snarky comment that put Maisie in her place, but this was still her place of business. She didn't want to make customers uncomfortable. If they were someplace else – anyplace else, really – Ivy would be all for an insult contest. "What do you want, Maisie?"

Maisie face flushed with incredulity. "You can't be serious," she grumbled. "If you even pretend that you don't know why I'm here … ."

"I have no idea why you're here," Ivy said, opting for honesty. "Unless … is this about your boots? I swear I wasn't aiming for them."

"That's an entirely different conversation," Maisie snapped. "I'm going to send you the bill for those boots, though. They cost more than you make in a year."

Ivy lifted her eyebrows but refused to rise to the bait. "I'm not paying for those boots," she said. "You can just wipe them off. Eggs and hash browns aren't known to be corrosive."

"Oh, you're paying for those boots."

"No, I'm not."

Maisie crossed her arms over her chest and scorched Ivy with a murderous look. "Yes, you are."

Ivy mimicked the pose. "No, I'm not."

"What's going on here?" Michael asked, Noah perched on his hip as he ambled over to the group. The toddler happily munched on a peanut butter cup while Michael fixed Maisie with a hateful glare. "What are you doing here, Maisie?"

"She thinks I'm paying for those boots," Ivy replied. "She's on crack if she thinks that."

"No, she's not on crack," Max said. "She just enjoys showing people her crack."

"Max, shut your mouth," Michael warned, handing Noah to his mother as he locked gazes with Maisie. "No one is paying for those boots, young lady. If that's why you're here, you can just skedaddle your skinny butt home. It's not going to happen."

"My boots are ruined," Maisie hissed.

"Your reputation is ruined, too," Michael pointed out. "I don't see you rushing out to make anyone pay for that."

Ivy snorted as she attempted to cover her mouth. She couldn't remember ever witnessing her father being openly rude, especially to a woman.

"Those boots are Italian leather," Maisie said. "They were expensive."

"Well, I'm Michigan proud and I don't give a rat's ass," Michael said. "Ivy was sick and the story I was told made you look like a fool. If I were you, I'd let it go."

"Well, you're not me."

"And my reputation isn't nearly as tarnished," Michael said, remaining calm. "No one is paying for those boots. If that's your sole reason for being here, go. No one cares about your complaints. In fact, if you want to lodge a complaint, we have a complaint booth you can visit."

"We do?" Ivy knit her eyebrows together. "Where?"

"It's about five miles into the woods," Michael said, extending his arm. "If you start walking now, you might get there before I put my boot in your behind."

Max widened his eyes to comical proportions as he locked gazes with Ivy and mouthed the word "wow." Ivy was equally flummoxed.

"Well, that just shows what you know," Maisie sniffed, shuffling from one foot to the other. "I'm not here about the boots – although I'm not going to just let that go."

"You'd better," Michael said. "If you're not here about the boots, why are you here?"

"Because of her," Maisie said, pointing at Ivy. "She's ruining my life."

Ivy's mouth dropped open. "Me? What did I do?"

"You know what you did," Maisie seethed. "I know what you did, too. It's all around town. Jack and Brian are looking to question the person dating Jeff Johnson … and you pointed them to me."

"I did not," Ivy argued. "I didn't even find out about you and Jeff Johnson until five minutes ago."

"Ha! You just admitted it!"

"Admitted what?" Ivy felt as if she was trapped on a speeding carousel with no hope of getting off. "I just told you I didn't know about the affair until a few minutes ago, so there was no way I could've been the one to rat you out."

"You're lying!"

"And you're a skank," Ivy shot back, not caring in the least that a few customers were staring her way. "I didn't tell anyone because I didn't know. I was going to tell Jack, don't get me wrong, but it looks as if that's not going to be necessary because he already knows. You can't blame me for this."

"Oh, I'm going to blame you," Maisie said. "You're trying to ruin my life. You've always been jealous of me and now you finally have your shot to drag me down."

"I don't need to drag you down because you do a fine job of that yourself."

"Oh, screw you."

"Screw you back."

Before Ivy realized what was happening, Maisie lashed out and slapped her across the face. The blow was so hard it caused Ivy to lean to the side. When she straightened, she was ticked. The fire in her eyes was Maisie's first clue that she'd made a mistake.

"I'm sorry," Maisie said, instantly contrite as she took a step back. "I didn't mean to do that. It was an accident."

"You'd better start running now," Ivy warned, extending a finger. "When I hit you, it's going to be a lot harder than that."

Maisie didn't need to be told twice. She turned on her heel and booked in the other direction. "Oh! I'm sorry!"

It was too late for that. Ivy was right behind her. "You're going to be sorry."

"WHAT happened?"

Jack hit the ground running when Brian pulled into the nursery's parking lot fifteen minutes later, meeting Max at the front gate.

Max tilted his head to the side. "Well … ."

Jack wasn't in the mood for games. "Is she hurt?"

"Oh, no," Max said, shaking his head. "She's great. She's invigorated even. Maisie Washington is another story."

"Maisie Washington?" Brian made a face as he walked around the front of the cruiser and joined Max and Jack. "We got a call about an incident involving a woman being thrown to the ground."

"Yes, that was Maisie," Max said. "She slapped Ivy and then Ivy took her to the ground."

"Oof." Brian wrinkled his nose. "She always was a tough little thing. I wanted to use her on my football team when you guys were in middle school, but the principal wouldn't let me because he was afraid she would get hurt."

"Yes, well, she's not hurt," Max said, his grin impish. "She's actually pretty proud of herself."

"Where is she?" Jack asked, craning his neck. He wasn't going to believe she was okay until he saw her with his own eyes.

"This way," Max said, leading Jack and Brian through the small crowd of curious onlookers. "Maisie only made it about ten feet before Ivy was on her. Ivy even gave her a headstart."

"I don't know what you're talking about," Jack said. "Are you saying Ivy actually tackled Maisie?"

Max smirked. "See for yourself."

Jack followed Max's finger, his eyes widening when he realized what he was looking at. Maisie was flat on the ground, prone, and Ivy sat on her back as she twisted Maisie's arm at the elbow and taunted her.

"Tell me you're sorry," Ivy ordered.

"I already said that," Maisie whined. "What else do you want me to do?"

"Tell her you're going to stop whining about those boots," Michael suggested, unwrapping another peanut butter treat and handing it to a happy Noah. For his part, the toddler didn't seem upset. He was more curious than anything else.

"I'm going to shut up about the boots," Maisie said, fighting against Ivy's grip. "Get off me, you cow!"

"What the hell is going on?" Jack strode in the direction of the women, taking a moment to survey them – and feel a small thrill of delight given how beautiful Ivy looked – before wrapping his arm around Ivy's waist and lifting her off Maisie.

"I'm not done," Ivy complained.

"You're done," Jack said, placing her on the ground and pushing a strand of her wild hair out of her face. "What are you even doing here? You told me you were going to be downtown all day."

"No, I told you I was going to be doing festival stuff all day," Ivy clarified. "I did my work downtown and now it's time to get the greenhouse in order for the haunted house. I told you about that two weeks ago."

"I guess I didn't realize you were doing that today," Jack said, instinctively pressing his hand to Ivy's forehead to make sure she wasn't running a fever. She was flushed, but she looked exhilarated rather than sick. "Why were you sitting on Maisie?"

"Because she's evil," Maisie answered, disdain practically dripping from her tongue as she rolled to a sitting position and dusted off her elbows. "I'm going to make you pay for this, you … witch."

"Shut up," Brian ordered, pressing the heel of his hand to his forehead. "Does someone want to tell me what is going on?"

"I will," Max said, his arm shooting into the air.

"I'm going to regret this, but go for it," Brian said, shaking his head.

"Ivy made me come here to help her with the greenhouse even though I already put in a hard day's work," Max began.

"Tell the story faster than that, Max," Brian ordered.

"We were standing here and I mentioned I heard a rumor about Jeff Johnson seeing someone and it happened to be Maisie," Max said. "Then she stormed in our direction and started yelling at Ivy.

"At first we thought it was because of the boots," he continued. "Dad put a kibosh on that and told Maisie she was a skank."

"I'm pretty sure I didn't use that word," Michael said dryly.

"You did in my memory," Max said. "When I tell the story down at the bar later, you're going to use it multiple times. Anyway, Maisie accused Ivy of telling Jack that she was having an affair with Jeff and Ivy said she just found out, but she was going to tell Jack because they make googly eyes at one another twenty-four hours a day. Maisie reacted by smacking Ivy and then running like a terrified girl. Ivy tackled her and after watching for five minutes, I told someone to call you guys."

"Oh, is that all?" Brian was flabbergasted. "Ivy Morgan, you're a grown woman. What are you doing attacking someone else?"

Ivy had the grace to lower her eyes and be embarrassed. "She started it."

"And you finished it," Max said, shooting Ivy a thumbs-up. "It was awesome. I even took photos on my phone."

Jack rubbed his cheek as he glanced between Ivy and Maisie, unsure how to proceed. He was on dangerous ground since Ivy was his girlfriend. He worried he might not be able to protect her if Maisie pressed charges.

"Well, no harm was done," Brian said.

"No harm?" Maisie was incensed. "She tackled me into the dirt. I'm going to sue."

"If you do that, I'm going to arrest you for assault," Brian said, catching Maisie off guard. "You did hit her first, after all."

"And threatened her after she was sick," Michael added. "We all saw it."

"But … ." Maisie made a disgusted face. "I hate you people."

"That's too bad," Brian said. "We're thrilled to see you. We've been looking for you for the past hour."

"Oh, she knew that," Max offered. "She was hiding."

"Shut up, Max!" Maisie exploded, earning a warning look from Brian. "What? He started it."

"And I'm going to finish it," Brian said. "I think you should come to the station with us, Maisie. We need to discuss a few things with you regarding your relationship with Jeff Johnson."

"Oh, what does it matter now?" Maisie complained. "Everything is out in the open. Everyone knows."

"Everyone knows what?" Jack pressed.

"Everyone knows that Jeff and I were together and he was going to leave his wife," Maisie replied. "There. Are you happy?"

"Not even remotely," Jack said. "You knew he was married, right?"

Maisie shrugged. "So?"

"You also knew he was about to become a father," Brian pointed out. "How did you think that was going to work out for you?"

"It's not my fault Karen trapped him with a baby," Maisie said, crossing her arms over her chest. "Jeff was a victim … and so was I. Our love was eternal."

"You're more like the perpetrator," Brian said. "Karen is the victim."

"They were also married for two years before Karen got pregnant," Ivy challenged. "She didn't trap him. You're the trap … the death trap."

"More like a herpes trap," Max said, jumping back when Maisie lashed out and tried to smack him. "What did I say?"

"That will be enough of that," Brian said, grabbing Maisie's arm and directing her toward the parking lot. "You need to come to the station with us. We have a lot to discuss."

"Fine," Maisie said. "I don't care where you take me as long as it's away from these crazy people."

"Duly noted," Jack said, shifting his eye back to Ivy. "Are you okay."

"I'm great." Ivy's smile was serene. "I feel like a million bucks."

"That's good," Jack said, kissing her cheek. "That means you'll be able to bribe me for a truce when we fight later tonight."

Ivy's smile slipped. "Are we really going to fight?"

"Don't worry. It will just be a small one." Jack squeezed her hand before moving to follow Brian to the parking lot, pausing in front of Max when something occurred to him. "Email me copies of those photos."

It took Max a moment to realize what he was referring to. "You're such a pervert."

Jack shrugged, unbothered. "She really was cute."

"I'll send them right away."

Nine

"We need to know when you last saw Jeff."

Maisie was easy to get into the police cruiser, but she was a bear when Jack and Brian got her back to the station. A few minutes of stewing in the back seat was all it took to get her juices flowing.

"I think I want a lawyer," Maisie said, reclining in the chair across Jack and Brian as she settled at the conference room table. "No, I definitely want a lawyer."

"You're not under arrest," Brian pointed out.

"Then you can't hold me."

"We're not holding you," Brian said. "If you want us to hold you, though, I'm sure Jack can get Ivy on the phone. My guess is that she'll be more than willing to fill out a report regarding the assault."

"Assault? She's the one who assaulted me," Maisie said, her eyes flashing.

"If we question the people at the nursery, how many of them are going to take your side over Ivy's?" Brian challenged. "I'm guessing it's not a lot."

Maisie's eyes reflected defeat as she heaved out a sigh and tossed her long hair over her shoulder. "Oh, good grief. You guys are real jerks. You know that, right?"

"I know that you're trying my patience," Brian said. "I repeat again, when was the last time you saw Jeff?"

"Two days ago," Maisie replied, her bitterness palpable. "We had a picnic lunch in the basement of the library."

"Was that because you didn't want anyone to know you were sleeping with a married man?" Jack asked.

"Oh, don't be like that," Maisie said. "You sound jealous."

"I'm pretty sure that 'jealous' is one of those words only people who don't understand what it really means toss about," Jack countered. "Why else would you have a picnic in the library basement?"

"Fine," Maisie muttered. "Yes. We ate lunch – and did other things – in the basement of the library three days a week."

"When did you start seeing each other?" Brian asked.

"About a month or so ago," Maisie answered. "He came into the library one day and we got to talking. One thing led to another … ."

"And you slept with a married man who was expecting a baby any day," Jack finished. "We get it."

"Ivy really has sucked the fun out of you," Maisie said. "Now that I'm free, I can fix that little problem if you're interested."

"I'm not even remotely interested."

"Yup. Ivy sucks," Maisie groused. "Is that all? Can I go?"

"Not even close," Brian said. "You said you saw Jeff two days ago at lunch. That was the day he died. The coroner is putting his death sometime in the early evening hours. Were you supposed to meet him that night?"

"No. We rarely met at night."

Brian knit his eyebrows together, confused. "If you rarely met at night, why would Jeff lie to his wife about being at the firehouse that night?"

"I … don't know," Maisie said, confused. "Did he really do that?"

Brian nodded. "Karen thought Jeff was at the station and Brad told us he was manning the station that night," he replied. "If that's the case, where was Jeff?"

"I honestly don't know," Maisie replied, shifting her jaw back and forth as she considered the possibilities associated with Brian's statement. "You don't think he was dating someone else, do you? I don't date cheaters."

Jack wanted to laugh – or at least lean over the table and throttle her. Instead, he kept his temper in check. "He was already a cheater," he said. "I guess it wouldn't be too much of a stretch to believe he had more than one person waiting to fill his nights."

"No, I guess not," Brian agreed. "I just … don't understand how he could've done this."

"Well, that makes two of us," Maisie said. "Trust me. When a man spends time with me, he leaves … fulfilled. There's no way Jeff was spending time with anyone else."

"He was obviously doing something with someone else," Jack pointed out. "He wasn't spending the night with you or his wife, and by all accounts, he wasn't needed at the station. What does that leave?"

Maisie was beside herself. "Well, he's just lucky he's dead," she said. "If he wasn't, I'd kill him myself."

Jack and Brian exchanged a dubious look.

"That brings me to my next question," Brian said. "Do you have an alibi for the night Jeff died?"

Instead of answering, Maisie slammed her hands on the table. "That's it! I want a lawyer."

And with that, the interview was over.

"WHAT ARE you doing, sweetheart?"

Michael found Ivy sorting through various Halloween lights in the greenhouse several hours later. He watched her for a few moments because she seemed lost in thought, finally deciding to approach the potential problem head-on rather than waiting for it to fester.

"Nothing," Ivy replied, jolting at her father's sudden appearance. "I'm just messing with the lights."

"You looked as if you were in a different world," Michael pointed out, shuffling to the middle of the floor and sitting cross-legged across from his only daughter. "What were you thinking about?"

"Quite a few things actually," Ivy admitted, offering her father a rueful smile. "The biggest is Jeff and Karen. Why do you think he was sleeping with Maisie when he already had a family?"

"I can't answer that," Michael replied. "I have no idea what he was thinking either. I've always been a proponent of divorce over infidelity."

"Have you ever considered cheating on Mom?"

Michael balked. "Your mother is the love of my life, Ivy," he said. "I have no reason – or urge, for that matter – to cheat on her."

"That's what I thought, but I wanted to hear it from you," Ivy said, unraveling a string of lights and pushing it to the side before reaching for another. "Do you think people are meant to be together?"

Michael answered without hesitation. "Yes."

"Do you think you and Mom were meant to be together?"

"Yes." Michael bobbed his head. "I don't really think you're asking about Mom and me, though. I think you're asking about Jack and you, and this is your roundabout way of getting to the subject."

Ivy lowered her eyes, sheepish. "You always could see right through me."

"That's a father's gift," Michael said, smiling. "Tell me what's really bothering you. Is it Jack? Are you afraid that Jack will somehow end up like Jeff?"

"I don't know," Ivy admitted. "I never thought Jeff would end up like Jeff. In my heart, I know Jack wouldn't cheat on me. It's just … frustrating … because I thought Jeff wouldn't cheat on Karen. Maybe that says something about my intuition."

"Maybe," Michael agreed. "I think it says more about Jeff's strength of character than anything else, though. Jeff was obviously weak and Maisie is a predator. We've always known that.

"Now, I don't want to take the onus of the blame off of Jeff because he was the one who made the vows and broke them, but Maisie probably took advantage of him," he continued. "When you're facing the birth of your first child, it's easy to get scared and do something stupid. That is a terrifying time and it's easy to get overwhelmed."

"You didn't."

"No, but I don't think of myself as weak either," Michael pointed out. "Jeff obviously wasn't a strong man and now his legacy is going to be cheating on his pregnant wife. We can't change that. It is what it is."

"I guess I just can't wrap my head around it," Ivy said. "I want to believe that people are inherently good. I want to believe that true love will win out."

"True love *always* wins out," Michael said. "It did for me. It will for you and Jack. I have faith."

Ivy was floored by the simple declaration. "Jack and I … I mean, we haven't said those words to each other."

"That doesn't mean you don't feel them," Michael said. "Ivy, you've always been my more difficult child. You're lovely and sweet when you want to be, but you're stubborn and mulish at other times."

"Thanks, Dad."

Michael ignored the sarcasm. "Every time I look at you when Jack is in the room, I feel the love," he said. "I feel the same thing from Jack. I spent years worrying you would find the wrong man. Then I spent years worrying you would find the right man. Then I spent years worrying you would never find someone who could tame that wild heart of yours. Jack did that, and I will be forever grateful."

Ivy pressed her lips together, her father's naked emotion causing her heart to warm. "What if Jack never says it?"

Michael chuckled, delighting in her minor bout of insecurity. "He'll say it."

"But … how do you know?"

"Because he feels it and the words will pour out when he can't contain them any longer," Michael replied. "He's as stubborn as you are. You're a good match for each other. I can't wait to see how all of this plays out."

"Are you sure we're going to get a happy ending?"

"Positive." Michael pushed himself to his feet and patted the top of Ivy's head. "If you guys want to pick up the pace, though, I would love a grandchild. That Noah is a pip. I want one of those of my own to spoil rotten."

Ivy's cheeks colored as she averted her gaze. "I'll keep that in mind."

"That's all I ask."

"HELLO, Karen."

This time when approaching the grieving widow, Brian internally vowed to be succinct and to the point. When the woman answered the front door of her house, though, his courage fled. She looked wrecked, for lack of a better word.

"Come in," Karen said tiredly, her hand resting on her stomach as she led Jack and Brian into her living room. It looked as if a tornado had struck. There were clothes and empty food containers strewn in every direction. "Sorry about the mess, but ... I'm honestly not sorry about the mess. I don't care about the mess."

"We don't care about the mess either," Jack said, sitting on one of the chairs across from the couch as Brian settled next to Karen. "We understand that you've got other things on your mind."

"Yes, like my dead husband," Karen said hollowly. "Are you here to tell me you've made an arrest?"

"We're here to ask you a few more questions," Brian replied. "We've been digging around and ... a few things have popped up."

"Oh, well, I don't like the sound of that," Karen said, leaning back on the couch dejectedly. "Let me guess: You heard Jeff was messing around and you want to know if it's true. Am I right?"

Jack knew he shouldn't be surprised by the woman's matter-of-fact tone, but he couldn't believe how blasé she was. "You knew?"

"Shadow Lake is a tiny town," Karen explained. "I knew almost before Jeff started sleeping with the town tramp."

"Why didn't you say anything?" Brian prodded. "You had to know that would be an important avenue for our investigation."

"I guess I hoped his death had nothing to do with that … slut … and everything to do with something else," Karen said. "It's not like I don't know that people were gossiping about me. I heard the whispers. A few people were even decent enough to tell me to my face that Jeff was messing around."

"Did you confront him?" Jack asked.

"No."

"Why not?"

"Because … ." Karen broke off, helpless. "What was I supposed to do? I'm going to have a baby and I have no job skills. It's not like I could kick him out of the house and get a do-over. I hoped he would get it out of his system and come back to me. Once I lost the baby weight … and could have sex again … I figured he would shape up.

"I mean, he's a man," she continued. "He has urges and I couldn't fulfill them because I'm so big. It wasn't his fault."

Jack felt inexplicably sad for the woman – and offended for her gender at the same time. He couldn't imagine being so defeated that you would sit by and watch the person you purportedly love walk all over you.

"Karen, where were you two nights ago?" Brian asked.

Karen jerked at the question, surprise washing over her features as she leveled her gaze on Brian. "Seriously?"

"We have to ask," Brian said. "We need to rule you out so we can focus on other people."

"Well, how exciting," Karen drawled. "I'm a murder suspect to boot. This week just keeps getting better and better."

Jack pursed his lips as he regarded her. She was clearly numb and putting on a show. "Where is your family? Why are you here alone?"

"Because I told them I needed some space and kicked them out," Karen said. "I kept seeing those 'poor her' looks when I entered a room. Conversation was going before I arrived and it came to a dead stop when they saw me. I knew what they were talking about. I just ... need a little time."

"I understand that," Jack said. "You still shouldn't be alone ... especially in your condition."

"I have a phone to call an ambulance if I go into labor," Karen said. "As for the rest ... I'm fine. I need to get used to taking care of myself. No one else is going to do it."

"Things will get better with time, Karen," Brian said. "I really need to record your alibi, though."

"I have no alibi," Karen said. "I was here alone. I thought Jeff was at the firehouse. Before you ask, I really thought he was there. I knew about his nooners with Maisie, but he kept saying he had to make up time at the firehouse if I expected him to be around once the baby was born. I didn't know I was going to need an alibi for my husband's murder. I'm sorry."

"Don't worry about it," Brian said, shaking his head. "In your condition, you could've hardly carried out the deed. We'll be in touch if we get any information."

"Great," Karen intoned, her voice hollow. "Information will make everything better. Information will give my baby a father. Information will make my life complete."

Brian exchanged a helpless look with Jack before getting to his feet. "We'll be in touch."

"I'm looking forward to it."

Ten

"Hey, honey."

Jack was exhausted when he returned to Ivy's house with a pizza in hand. He expected to find her inside. When he didn't, frustration overwhelmed him until he realized she was probably still at the greenhouse. Instead of stomping over to the property to collect her, he packed a picnic and grabbed a blanket before joining her. He was determined to ensure a pleasant evening.

"Hi." Ivy lifted her eyes toward the window to her right, surprised by his sudden appearance and the growing shadows on the other side of the glass. "What time is it?"

"Almost six."

"I'm so sorry," Ivy said, hopping down from the chair she was standing on. "I got caught up in what I was doing and lost track of time."

"I figured," Jack said, placing his food goodies on the counter before opening the blanket and resting it on the floor. "That's why I came to you."

"Are you angry?"

"Not at you."

"Are you angry at someone else? If so, please tell me it's Maisie."

Jack was in no mood for a rousing game of Twenty Questions, but he couldn't help but smile at his girlfriend's fervent expression. "I'm angry with the situation, not with a particular person."

"Oh." Ivy shuffled closer to Jack and opened her arms. "Do you need a hug?"

"Oh, so cute," Jack said, pulling her to him and tightening his arms around her waist. "I do need a hug. It just so happens I need it from you, too. How did you know?"

"Perhaps I'm psychic."

"I'm not ruling it out," Jack said, pressing a soft kiss to her mouth before releasing her. "I got pizza, breadsticks, and those cinnamon things you like."

"You're a very good provider," Ivy said, settling on the blanket next to Jack and smiling as he set the bountiful feast on the floor. "We could've gone back to the house, though. It might be more comfortable."

"I'm fine here," Jack said, glancing around. The greenhouse looked nothing like it had when he was inside a few weeks before. "You've been busy."

"I didn't do all of this," Ivy said, her stomach growling when she opened the pizza box. She had no idea how hungry she was until the scent of food wafted through the room. "Jessica stayed and helped for a few hours. My dad was happy to take Noah off her hands. Max was a big help, too. Well, he was a big help as soon as he stopped talking about my fight with Maisie."

"Ah, Maisie," Jack clucked, leveling his gaze on Ivy. "Do you want to talk about that now or wait until after dinner?"

"Now," Ivy replied, not missing a beat as she grabbed a slice of pizza from the veggie side of the circle. "I don't want it hanging over my head if you're going to yell."

"I'm not going to yell," Jack said. "I'm just ... I don't even know what to say. I never expected to find you sitting on top of another woman in the middle of your nursery."

"It wasn't one of my finer moments," Ivy admitted. "I just … couldn't seem to stop myself. I've put up with a lot of crap over the years where she's concerned. I've even put up with her hitting on you. When she slapped me, though, I think I saw red and wanted to kill her."

"Uh-huh." Jack used his finger to tip Ivy's face to the side so he could study her features under the limited light. "I don't think it's going to leave a mark."

"I wish I would've left a mark on her."

"Well, she's dealing with her own issues," Jack said. "Before we get to that, though, I would prefer that you be much more careful – perhaps not pick a fight at all – the next time you end up in the hospital. Do you think you can do that?"

"I don't know. I didn't mean to do it this time."

"I guess that's the best you can offer," Jack said, shaking his head. "The sad thing is that you looked adorable in those photos."

Ivy scowled. "I cannot believe that Max sent those to you. I threatened to take away his pumpkin cookies if he did it. I guess that means you're getting all of the pumpkin cookies."

Jack grinned. "He told me you were going to punish him. I offered to give him half of my cookies."

"No way!"

"Sorry, honey," Jack said. "The photos were totally worth it. You looked … smoking hot."

"Oh, well, it's hard for me to be angry when you're being so charming," Ivy said, giggling as she leaned her head against Jack's shoulder and took another huge bite. "What did Maisie say?"

Jack made a face. "Do you have to talk with your mouth full?"

"Do you want to pick a fight?"

"Absolutely not," Jack replied. "I'm too tired for a fight. As for Maisie, she's a real piece of work. With one breath she told us Jeff was going to leave his wife and marry her. With the next she made it sound as if they only met up in the afternoon a few times a week and it wasn't much of a relationship. I don't know what to believe."

"It could be both."

"How so?"

"Maisie doesn't understand about a real relationship," Ivy explained. "She's never been in one. Spending a month having nooners with Jeff probably was the longest she's ever been with a man. To her, he might've seemed like he was going to leave Karen."

"And what do you think?"

Ivy shrugged. "My dad thinks that Maisie preyed on Jeff when he was feeling extremely vulnerable because he was terrified about becoming a father," she said. "I think Jeff was a jackhole of the royal variety, but I have no doubt Maisie twisted his head. Maybe Jeff thought it was just a fling and he'd be able to somehow salvage his marriage."

"That's certainly what Karen thought," Jack said. "She thought once she dropped the baby weight that Jeff would come running home."

Ivy was horrified. "She knew?"

"She knew."

"But … why didn't she say something?"

"We asked her that very question, but she didn't have a compelling answer," Jack replied. "All she said was that she didn't have any job prospects and couldn't afford to let go of her marriage. She thought Jeff would see the error of his ways."

"That's terrible." Ivy thoughtfully chewed on her pizza as she watched Jack out of the corner of her eye. "You wouldn't do that, right?"

Jack, his hand in the box to snag another slice of pizza, stilled. "Are you asking me if I would ever cheat on you?" He couldn't help being a little insulted.

"I believe you wouldn't," Ivy said. "I also believed Jeff wouldn't, too. I'm starting to wonder if my head is screwed up."

Jack chuckled, alleviating some of the tension in the room. "I would never cheat on you. I have no inclination to cheat on you. You're more than enough. Sometimes I think you're too much. You're still the only person I want."

Ivy smiled at the admission. "Me, too."

"You're the only person you want?"

"No, you're the only person I want," Ivy clarified. "I knew you wouldn't cheat on me. I'm just not sure I can trust my head right now. It seems … messed up. I swear, when I went after Maisie today, it was as if someone else was controlling me."

"Well, I don't have a lot of sympathy for Maisie," Jack said. "She earned whatever you threw at her. As for the rest, I happen to like your head the way it is. Sure, you can do some amazing things that other people can't, but that doesn't make me adore you any less."

"That was absolutely charming."

Jack winked. "I try."

"So, what are we doing after dinner?" Ivy asked, staring at Jack through lowered lashes. "Do you want me to give you a tour of the greenhouse?"

Jack was intrigued by the suggestion. "Is this place heated? The second the sun goes down, things are going to get chilly."

"I have a heater."

"How about you give me a brief tour and then we head back to the house," Jack suggested. "I'll start a fire and rub your back before letting the night – and possibly our dreams – take us somewhere special."

"Oh, do you want to dream walk?" Ever since discovering they could enter each other's dreams, the couple made it a habit to book dates several times a week. They refrained from doing it every night, though, because sometimes normal rest held its own appeal.

"I do," Jack confirmed. "I was thinking we could go to a sunny beach since we won't see one in real life for months."

"I was thinking we could go to a British castle and do it on a bear-skinned rug," Ivy countered.

Jack barked out a laugh. "You're an animal rights activist."

"It's not a real rug."

"Sold," Jack said, dusting off his hands before reaching for another slice of pizza. "I think I'm going to need to carb up if I want to keep up with you tonight."

"I think you're exactly right."

"I CAN'T do it with the bear staring at me." Ivy locked gazes with the imagined bear rug and frowned. "This is so not how I thought this would go."

"This is exactly how I thought this would grow," Jack grumbled. He was shirtless in the dreamscape and he rolled over on the rug and stared at the ceiling. The fake bear didn't bother him in the slightest. "Can't you turn it into a mattress or something?"

Ivy shrugged. "I'm not magic."

"You're definitely magic," Jack argued.

After finishing their picnic and a brief tour of the greenhouse, Ivy and Jack walked back to her house with their fingers linked and their hearts and stomachs full. They spent an hour in front of the fire watching television – Jeff Johnson's murder was the top story on the local news – and then they retired early.

They didn't go to sleep right away – they enjoyed joining in the physical world as much as the dreamscape – and when they finally did drift off, they agreed to meet in the English countryside. That was thirty minutes ago and Jack was about to lose his patience.

"Ivy, let's go someplace else," Jack suggested. "The countryside castle was a lovely idea. The bear rug was not. Even if you somehow manage to trade it out, you won't be able to get it out of your head. Let's go to the beach."

"But … I wanted to hang out here," Ivy whined. "This is much more weather appropriate."

"Cold weather."

"And we're going to be living in cold weather ourselves in a few weeks," Ivy pointed out. "I was just getting us in the mood."

"Honey, I'm always in the mood," Jack said, snagging her around the waist and rolling her so she could sit on his stomach. "Pick another spot. We'll revisit the castle with fluffy synthetic rugs next time. I promised."

"Okay." Ivy didn't look thrilled with Jack's suggestion, but she knew he was right. She wouldn't be able to put the poor bear's expression out of her mind if they didn't switch locales. "Do you want a white sand beach?"

"Surprise me."

"How about you surprise me?" Ivy suggested. Jack could pick locations when he put effort into it. More often than not he let Ivy choose where she wanted to go – he was simply happy to be with her – but he was responsible for the occasional shared dream.

"Okay. I think I'm up for that."

"You'd better be." Ivy leaned over and kissed him before straightening. "Giddyap."

"Oh, now there's an idea," Jack said. "We're going to go to a beach where we can watch wild horses. Just you wait."

"I'm so excited." Ivy smiled as Jack disappeared from beneath her, sucking in a breath as she waited for his heart to call to hers. He was already in the new dreamscape. She just had to find him. Unfortunately for her, something else caught her attention in the castle hallway before that could happen.

"What the … ?"

Ivy slowly got to her feet when she saw the dark figure watching her from the darkened narrow expanse. She recognized the man right away, although his face was red and his neck bent at an odd angle.

"Jeff?"

"I don't want to die."

Ivy licked her lips as she glanced around, unsure what was happening. She instinctively pressed her hand to her forehead, but her temperature was normal. Of course, since she wasn't really here, she rationalized that she could be making up the temperature reading in her head.

"Do you know who killed you, Jeff?"

The man stared at her, his eyes plaintive. "I don't want to die."

Ivy was filled with sympathy, but the broken record was starting to grate. "You're already dead."

"I don't want to die."

"Say something else!" Ivy exploded, gripping her hands together as Jeff took an uncertain step toward her. "And stay over there."

She had no idea what to expect from a dreamscape vision, but she didn't want to risk the man touching her. If she could interact with Jack – really feel him – she couldn't help but wonder what would happen should Jeff touch her. She honestly didn't want to find out.

"I don't want to die."

"I don't know what to say to you," Ivy said, swallowing hard. "You're already dead, Jeff. I don't know if you're caught in a loop … or if you're trying to show me something … or if I'm seeing you from someone else's memory. I don't know how to help you."

"I don't want to die." Jeff lurched forward, reaching out with his grayish hand as he attempted to hold on to something real. Ivy tried to evade him, but he was quicker than he should've been. He latched onto her wrist and held firm. "I don't want to die!" He screamed the words, causing Ivy to wrench her arm away from him.

In her haste to get away from the ghost, she tripped over the bear's head and tumbled to the ground. Jeff continued moving forward as Ivy's heart rate sped up. She couldn't think of what else to do, she called for the only man who could help her.

"Jack!"

IVY bolted awake in the bed, her body dripping with sweat as she sucked in huge mouthfuls of oxygen. Jack was instantly alert at her side.

"Where were you?"

"I didn't leave the castle," Ivy gritted out, running her hand over her forehead. "Do I feel hot to you?" She didn't want to panic Jack, but she couldn't seem to rein in her emotions.

Jack pressed his hand to her forehead … and then his lips. "You feel normal to me. Do you feel hot?"

"I don't know," Ivy said, her voice cracking. "I … ."

"It's okay," Jack soothed, wrapping his arms around her and pressing her head to his chest. "Tell me what happened."

"You left and I was waiting for you to drag me into the dreamscape," Ivy said. "Then Jeff was there … and he kept saying he didn't want to die. Then he grabbed my arm and I tripped over the stupid bear head."

Jack felt lost. "Do you think that was real?"

"I don't know. I mean … it was a dream. It couldn't have been real, right?"

Jack wasn't sure, but he had no intention of frightening her. She was already at her limit. "I think it was a dream," he said. "I think I took too long calling you to me and you fell into regular sleep. It's okay."

"I don't want to go back to the castle."

"We're not going anywhere," Jack said, reclining on the mattress and pulling Ivy on top of him so he could tuck the covers around her shaking body. "We're going to stay right here. I won't let anyone into your dreams for the rest of the night. I promise."

"You can't make that promise."

"Watch me."

Eleven

Ivy's mind was muddled when she woke, and when she shifted her chin she found Jack watching her. His eyes didn't look sleepy, which meant he'd been up – but silent and still so as not to wake her – for at least several minutes.

"Morning."

"Morning, honey," Jack said, smoothing her hair and kissing her forehead. "How do you feel?"

The previous evening's nightmare came crashing back, and in the bright light of day Ivy felt silly for freaking out. "I'm sorry I acted like a baby last night."

"You didn't act like a baby," Jack countered. "You had a nightmare. You're allowed to be vulnerable occasionally. You know that, right?"

Ivy worked her mouth as she tried to decide how to respond. Jack filled the conversational gap before she could.

"My main function is to take care of you and ward off bad dreams," he said. "That's what I did last night."

"You *did* do it," Ivy said, realization washing over her as she lifted her head so it was easier to lock gazes with Jack. "You said you were going to keep the dreams away and you did it."

"I … ." Jack had no idea what she was talking about.

"How did you do it?" Ivy was genuinely curious.

"How did I do what?" Jack asked, pushing her flyaway hair away from her face. If someone told him a year before he would be completely besotted with a

Bohemian beauty who boasted pink streaks in her hair, he would've had the person locked up for lunacy. Now he couldn't imagine being away from her for more than a few hours.

"You kept the dream away," Ivy replied. "I was convinced I wouldn't be able to fall asleep again because of that nightmare, but you said you were going to make sure I didn't have a bad dream. I didn't think that was possible … but I didn't dream at all."

"Oh, *that*," Jack intoned, rolling his eyes. She was giving him more power than he could lay claim to. That didn't mean he wouldn't take the credit if it meant he got a little morning action as a reward. "I just used the incredible power of my mind and created a tapestry of strength so I could put it over your mind – kind of like a blanket – and we both slept heavy."

Ivy's face was unreadable as she stared at him. "Are you making that up?"

Jack shrugged. "I don't know why you didn't dream, honey," he said. "I was determined to make sure you felt safe enough to sleep, but I think I might've dozed off before you did. I'm sorry about that."

"I didn't dream, though," Ivy mused. "I always dream."

"Well, maybe the dream from earlier was bad enough to cause your subconscious to shun dreaming," Jack suggested. "I'm not sure the answer is as important as your health, though. You don't feel sick, right? If you feel as if you're going to relapse, we should get you to the clinic now."

"I don't feel sick," Ivy said. "I do remember touching my face to see if I was hot in the dream, though.

Then I realized that was stupid because it wasn't real and I couldn't actually touch myself."

"You need to stop talking about touching yourself, because it's giving me ideas," Jack said, cupping the back of her head and resting his lips against her forehead. "You feel normal. Not hot at all."

Ivy feigned outrage. "Thanks."

"You know what I mean," Jack chided, shaking his head. "You're so much work sometimes."

"Yes, but I'm worth it."

"You're definitely worth it," Jack said, snuggling closer as he glanced at the clock on the nightstand. He would have to hop in the shower relatively soon if he wanted to make it to work on time. "What are your plans for the day?"

"I'm working in the greenhouse."

"Is your father going to be at the nursery?"

Ivy cocked a challenging eyebrow. "Are you insinuating that I need my father to babysit me?"

"I'm insinuating that I don't want you to be alone after you were so sick," Jack replied. "I'm allowed to worry about you so don't even think of picking a fight."

"I would never pick a fight," Ivy intoned, purposely widening her eyes to feign innocence. "I'm a good girl."

Jack didn't want to smile, but he couldn't help himself. "You're my good girl," he said, tickling her ribs and delighting in the way she gasped and giggled. "Promise me you'll stay close to the greenhouse today."

"I can't," Ivy sputtered.

"Promise me," Jack prodded.

"I can't," Ivy repeated, trying to skirt away from his hands but failing. His arms were too long and he was much stronger than her. They both knew it. "What if I have to run to town because I need lights … or decorations … or apples for my pies?"

Jack ceased his finger ministrations and regarded Ivy with a curious look. "What pies?"

"I should've known you would latch onto that part of the conversation."

"Yes, well, you know how I feel about pie," Jack said, rubbing his nose against her cheek. "Why are you making pie?"

"Because I always make apple and pumpkin pies for the festival."

"Pies … plural?" Jack was intrigued.

"Oh, I see where this is going," Ivy said. "You want to make a deal. Okay. I promise to make you an apple pie all your own if you promise to stop hovering."

"No deal."

Jack's succinct response caught Ivy off guard. "No deal?"

"Nothing will ever make me stop worrying about you," Jack said. "I am not physically capable of picking pie over you."

"But … you love my apple pie."

"And yet somehow you're more important," Jack said, his eyes twinkling. "I'm *literally* incapable of ceasing the hovering."

Ivy scowled. "You know I hate it when you use that word."

"That's why I used it."

Ivy blew out a sigh. "Fine. If I promise to take my dad or Max into town with me if I need to go, then will you stop hovering?"

"Probably not," Jack replied. "I will feel better about you working all day if you do that, though."

"Well … I guess you have your deal."

"Not quite," Jack said, grabbing Ivy's waist when she tried to wiggle away. "I want a little … added enticement … on my end if we're going to agree to this deal."

Ivy pressed her lips together. "Oh, really? I thought you were going to be late for work."

Jack smacked his lips to Ivy's and drew her in for an extended kiss, a surge of heat washing over both of them before he pulled back his head. "You're also more important than work."

"That was a good answer."

"I do my best."

"YOU LOOK … all shiny and happy this morning."

Brian met Jack in the funeral home parking lot shortly before ten, a dark look on his face. Instead of coming straight to the station, Jack texted and said he had to help Ivy with something – because she was still getting over being ill – and would be twenty minutes late. That twenty minutes turned into an hour – and then the meeting place changed locales when Brian got a call that Jeff and Karen's families were going to war at the funeral home. Jack's chipper countenance wasn't doing anything to alleviate Brian's bad mood.

"I'm sorry I'm late," Jack said, averting his gaze. "Ivy's stomach is still an iffy proposition and I had to make sure she got a bland breakfast in her before I could go."

"Uh-huh." Brian didn't believe that for a second. "Did you feed her yourself?"

"I just made sure she had food."

"Are you sure?" Brian challenged. "You're so codependent I can almost picture you feeding her … as if she was a little baby."

Jack made a disgusted face. "Ivy was very sick. I'm not sure that making fun of her is the right way to go … from a karma standpoint, I mean."

"Oh, son, you're so full of crap it's dangerous to flush because the pipes might get jammed," Brian said, the corners of his mouth tipping up despite his best efforts to the contrary. "We both know you weren't feeding Ivy … well, anything that can be talked about in polite circles, that is. I don't care that you were late because you were doing the love shack limbo. I care that you were late when we're working a murder case."

Jack stilled, a brief bout of shame washing over him. "You're right. I shouldn't have done that. It won't happen again."

Brian studied him for a moment and then chuckled. "We both know it's going to happen again. You can't help yourself. I'll let it go for today, though. We have bigger apples to bob this morning."

Jack tilted his head to the side. "Apples to bob?"

"My wife won't stop yammering about the festival and I've got apples on the brain because she runs the bobbing booth," Brian replied. "I'm sorry."

"Ivy is really excited for the festival, too. She's decking out the greenhouse and everything."

"She does that every year. It's a sight to behold."

"Well, as long as she's happy, I'm happy," Jack said. "What's the deal in here? Why are we calling on a funeral home?"

"Because apparently Dave Johnson and Don Merriman are about to throw punches."

"Who are Dave Johnson and Don Merriman?"

"Dave Johnson is Jeff Johnson's father. Don Merriman is Karen Johnson's father."

"Oh." Jack creased his forehead. "Oh!"

"Yes, there it is," Brian intoned. "We have two fighting families in the middle of a murder … which means we might have motives coming out of our ears in the next few minutes. Be on the lookout."

"YOUR SON was a piece of filth!"

Don Merriman stood in the center of the viewing room, his face red and his brow sweaty, and stared down Dave Johnson as two factions of the same extended family scurried away from the center of the storm.

"My son might not have been perfect, but neither is your daughter," Dave shot back. "If she was a better wife, none of this would've ever happened."

"You take that back."

"Suck my … ."

"Okay, that will be enough of that," Brian announced, stepping between the two men and placing his hands in the center of their chests to maintain distance. "Now, is this really the way you want to mourn your son, Dave?"

"My son was murdered, and I'm pretty sure she did it." Dave made the announcement in a theatrical manner and pointed at a disinterested Karen as she sat on a couch by the window. "I refuse to hold my tongue. She's a murderer."

"And your son was a philanderer," Don said. "If she did kill him, he deserved it."

"Thanks, Dad," Karen intoned, glancing around. "Does anyone want to get this kid out of me so I can have a drink? I would really like a drink."

"The second that kid comes out of you, we're suing for custody," Dave raged. "You'd better hold it in there as long as you can, because once he's out, he's going to be coming home with me. Then you can drink all you want. Heck, then you can drink yourself to death. You'd be doing us all a favor."

"You shut your hole!" Don exploded.

"I'm not shutting anything," Dave said. "I'm taking that kid. Mark my words."

Karen snorted. "How do you figure that?"

"Because you can't take care of a baby," Don replied. "You don't have a job and you have no means of financially supporting a baby."

"I'm sure I'll figure something out," Karen muttered.

"And I'm sure you won't be raising that baby because you'll be in prison for murdering my son!"

Jack wasn't familiar with the players, but he had no intention of letting a blustering fool like Dave Johnson attack a pregnant woman. "Knock it off," he ordered, burning Dave with a harsh look. "That's the mother of your grandchild."

"That woman doesn't mean a thing to me," Dave said, crossing his arms over his chest. "She killed my son."

"Oh, really?" Jack was in a good mood, but it wasn't likely to last if the screaming continued. Dave's tone alone irritated him. "How do you think she did that? She's about to give birth any day. Your son easily weighed a hundred and eighty pounds. How did she manage to get him up on a cross in her condition?"

Dave balked. "I … um … ." He obviously hadn't considered that part of the equation.

"Why would she kill him?" Brian pressed. "She was aware of her financial situation more than anyone. Wouldn't it make far more sense for her to ignore Jeff's infidelity to keep up appearances and a roof over her head?"

"I … ." Dave's cheeks colored.

"Oh, look. He's speechless. It's a miracle," Don said, clutching his hands together and staring at the ceiling. "Thank you, Lord."

"Knock that off," Brian warned, poking Don's arm to get his attention. "While we're chatting here, it sounds as if you knew Jeff was running around. Did you know before or after his death?"

"I've known for a month," Don replied. He wasn't shy in the least to offer up a motive for himself. "I've known since the first time it happened. Do you want to know how?"

Brian shrugged. "Sure."

"Because Maisie told anyone who would listen," Don said. "She's a slut and she doesn't care who knows it. Jeff had to want to get caught to sleep with her."

"Or get herpes," someone on the other side of the room quipped.

"That, too," Don said. "I've known from the beginning. I didn't know Karen knew – and I was honestly trying to keep it from her because she was so close to giving birth and I didn't want to endanger the baby – but I knew. Before you ask, I didn't kill him."

"Where were you three days ago?"

"Um … ." Don tapped his chin. "Oh! That was the day I had to run down to Grand Rapids to pick up the new living room couch. The store will have a record of when I picked it up. I left at around eleven that morning and didn't get back until about seven that night. After that I had dinner at the diner and recruited two guys to help me unload the couch before going home."

As far as alibis go, that was a fairly decent one in Jack's book.

"That doesn't mean he didn't do it," Dave argued. "He could be lying."

"We're going to check out everyone's alibis, Dave," Brian said. "For now, though, you guys need to knock this off. This is a time of mourning. Karen is about to have a baby and that's forever going to join together your families. You need to suck it up and stop being children."

Dave and Don eyed each other for a moment.

"I'm not sure that's possible," Dave said finally.

"I *know* it's not possible," Don added. "He's a snake … and he's been threatening my daughter."

"I'm going to take that baby," Dave spat.

"By the time we're done, you won't even know this baby's name," Don shot back.

Jack and Brian exchanged a dubious look as they tried to keep the two men from coming to blows. Now what?

Twelve

"Hello, darling daughter of mine."

Michael greeted Ivy with a bright smile as she entered the nursery, his eyes busy as they roamed her face. Her color was good, her smile welcoming, and she had almost an iridescent appeal as she waved at customers. She still seemed somehow … sad. That was the only word he could come up with to describe her.

"Hello, Father," Ivy said primly. "How are you this fine autumn day?"

"Ugh. I can already tell you're going to be a pain today," Michael said, sitting in his usual chair behind the counter. "You look very … ."

"Pretty?"

"You always look pretty," Michael said. "You're my prettiest child."

"I can't wait to tell Max."

"Max is my most handsome child," Michael clarified. "Boys aren't pretty."

"Jack is pretty."

"Does Jack know you refer to him as pretty?"

"Jack lets me refer to him however I want," Ivy replied, leaning her elbows on the countertop as she glanced around. "We're busy today."

"Enjoy it," Michael said. "In another month this place is going to be a ghost town."

"I know you don't believe it, but I actually enjoy the downtime," Ivy said. "It gives me a chance to work on my lotions and soaps without having to leave my house if the weather gets bad."

"You could always go to Florida with your mother and me. We never get snow down there."

"I ... ." Ivy pursed her lips. She knew he was messing with her, but she didn't want to hurt his feelings. "I have Nicodemus."

"Cats are allowed in Florida," Michael pointed out, his eyes full of mirth. "Are you sure Nicodemus is the only one you're worried about leaving?"

Ivy made an exaggerated "well, duh" face. "Fine. You caught me. I'm not leaving Jack. Are you happy?"

"Very," Michael replied, grinning. "I think you two are adorable."

"You do not."

"I do, too," Michael argued. "I can tell you're in quite the mood today. What's going on?"

"I'm not in a mood," Ivy clarified. "It's more that … I had a nightmare." She had no idea why she was opening up to her father, but she needed someone to talk to. With Jack and Max at work, she didn't have a lot of options.

Michael's eyes turned somber as sympathy washed over him. "Did you have a nightmare about finding Jeff's body and getting sick?"

"Kind of." Ivy rubbed her cheek and focused on the greenhouse, internally debating how much she should tell her father. "A few weird things have been happening since I met Jack."

"You mean the dream walking? Yeah. I heard about that."

Ivy was flabbergasted. She told Max … and Brian kind of knew, although he had no idea how it worked and seemed reluctant to explore it further … but she'd purposely kept it from her mother and father. The only other person who knew was her aunt.

"Aunt Felicity told you, didn't she?"

"I guess a little," Michael conceded. "Max let it slip when he was making fun of you and Jack for holing yourselves up in the house one weekend. He made it sound weirder than it was. Felicity was upset at his tone and she filled us in on the rest of it."

"Oh." Ivy wasn't used to feeling uncertain around her father. "What do you think of that?"

"I've always know you were magic. This just proves it."

"But … do you think it's weird?"

Michael shrugged. "Does it matter? It's happening, sweetheart. Whether it's a product of you and Jack growing close to one another or something else entirely, I honestly don't know. It doesn't sound as if you can change it, though, so you might as well enjoy it."

"We do a lot of the time," Ivy said. "We don't do it every night, though. Jack insists on regular sleep and dreams … and I think he's right. I don't want to get too dependent on sharing our relationship in the dreams."

"I think that sounds practical," Michael said. "So, what's the problem?"

"Well, last night we went to a castle," Ivy replied. "It was my idea and then I didn't like it because the bear rug kept staring at me."

Michael barked out a laugh. "Even in your dreams, you're difficult. How cute. Continue."

"Jack decided to pick a different location, and I was going to follow but … ."

"But what?"

"Jeff Johnson showed up."

Michael licked his lips as he glanced around, making sure no one was eavesdropping before continuing. "I need more details, Ivy. Was he alive or dead in the dream?"

"Both."

"I … ."

"He was dead," Ivy said. "Kind of like a zombie. His skin was gray and his neck was broken at an odd angle. I don't think his neck was broken, though. Jack didn't mention that."

"Does he tell you everything about his cases?"

"No."

"Well, then perhaps you should ask," Michael suggested. "Did Jeff say anything to you?"

"Just that he didn't want to die. He repeated it over and over again. It happened the other day in the corn maze, too."

Michael stilled. "You dreamed about Jeff when you passed out in the corn maze? I didn't know that."

"That's because I didn't tell anyone but Jack," Ivy said. "I don't want people looking at me as if I'm strange and odd. Of course, that's exactly how you're looking at me, so I guess I was right to be worried."

"That's not how I'm looking at you," Michael countered. "I'm trying to understand what you're saying. Did Jeff talk to you when you got sick in the corn maze?"

"No. I saw his foot and passed out. I woke up briefly in a dark room, although it turned white. I kept hearing someone say that he didn't want to die. I never saw a face and didn't know it was Jeff at the time. Then I woke up immediately and got sick. I felt as if I was on fire."

"And you told this to Jack?"

Ivy nodded.

"What did he say?"

"He said we would figure it out and not to worry," Ivy replied. "I wasn't worried until the dream last night. Jack played it off and told me that it was a regular nightmare and I shouldn't get worked up about it, but the more I think about it, the more I'm certain that I was still in the dreamscape when Jeff found me."

"I don't know what to think about this," Michael admitted, rubbing his chin.

Ivy's heart sank. "You don't believe me, do you?"

"It's not that I don't believe you," Michael clarified. "I have no basis for comparison so I can't even picture what you're describing. I believe you, though. Have you considered talking to your aunt about this? If anyone is going to understand what's going on, it has to be her."

"I don't know," Ivy hedged. "I promised Jack I would stay close today. I don't want to make a big deal out of it. What if it turns out to be nothing?"

"What if it turns out to be something?"

"I need to think," Ivy said, forcing the dour expression from her face and smiling at her father. "I'll be in the greenhouse."

"We're not done talking about this."

"We are for now," Ivy said. "I can't make a decision until I have time to think. I need to be alone to think. I won't be far if you need me."

"I think I'm the one who should be saying that," Michael grumbled.

"Fine." Ivy blew out a sigh. "You'll be close if I need you. Does that make you happy?"

"Not even close," Michael said. "I'm not in the mood to fight, though, so I'll give you the time you need."

"Thank you. That's all I ask."

IVY SPENT the next two hours working in the greenhouse, only taking a break when her shoulders started to ache and she wanted some fresh air. She stepped outside, inhaling deeply as she rolled her neck. She'd forgotten how much work she put into the haunted greenhouse each year. It was worth it, though.

Ivy trailed her fingers along the glass as she walked the length of the building. She wasn't in the right frame of mind to see other people but stretching her legs held a lot of appeal. In truth, she wanted to stretch her legs in the direction of her fairy ring. It was mostly empty this time of year – the mushrooms that formed the magical ring dead – but it was still her happy place. In a few weeks the snow would be too thick to visit it at all.

Ivy made up her mind on the spot. She'd promised Jack she wouldn't wander away without a chaperone, but the fairy ring was on her property and only a few minutes away. She could get there, spend a few minutes relaxing, and then get back without anyone noticing. Jack would be none the wiser.

Even though she knew she was breaking her promise, Ivy stepped into the thick foliage without a backward glance. She wasn't lying to her father when she said she needed time to think. She couldn't do that if her head wasn't in the right place, and the only place she wanted to be was the fairy ring.

So that's the direction she headed.

"WELL, well, well. Look what we have here."

Michael made a face when he saw Jack approaching the front counter shortly before noon. The police officer had three huge bags of food from the diner in his hands, and a wistful smile on his face. The smile slipped when he saw Michael.

"Mr. Morgan."

"I've told you to call me Michael."

"Michael," Jack said, his smile sheepish. "Is Ivy here?"

"That depends," Michael replied. "What's in those bags?"

Jack pursed his lips. He'd been hoping to surprise Ivy with lunch – and another greenhouse picnic – and make sure she was okay at the same time. He thought the picnic idea would make good cover. "A hamburger and fries for me. I got Ivy the veggie wrap and fries."

"Oh, that looks fun," Michael said. "You have three bags, though."

"I got cake for desert, too."

"Oh, you're so cute I just want to kiss you," Michael said, winking. "Do you have enough for me in there, too?"

"I … ." Jack's heart dropped. He was hoping for some alone time with Ivy. "Of course. You can have whatever you want."

Michael made a clucking sound with his tongue. "I can't say you don't have good manners, son," he said. "As for lunch, I brought my own. I was just messing with you."

Jack was secretly relieved. "Oh, well, we'll miss you."

"And there are those manners again." Michael was enjoying himself. "You have much better manners than Ivy."

"She just has a different way of expressing herself," Jack said. "Speaking of Ivy, where is she?"

"I think she's still in the greenhouse," Michael said, falling into step with Jack as they moved in that direction. "I'm going to check out there with you so I can mess with her – tell her I'm horning in on your lunch – and then I'll leave you to it."

Jack cast a sidelong look in Michael's direction. "I always wondered where Max got that sadistic streak of his when it comes to teasing Ivy. Now I realize he got it from you."

"Yeah, Max is a natural," Michael said, puffing out his chest as they reached the greenhouse. "Now, let me do the talking. Oh, Ivy! Jack bought the three of us lunch. We're going to have a cozy picnic together."

Jack swallowed his laughter as he followed Michael into the building, pulling up short when he realized Michael was standing in the middle of the room but there wasn't another human being in sight. "What's going on?"

"She's not here," Michael said. "I saw her go in here a few hours ago. I don't understand."

Even though he knew outright fear with nothing to back it up was unreasonable, Jack's stomach twisted. He tried to remain overtly calm as he placed the food bags on the counter. "When was the last time you saw her?"

"When she told me about the dreams – I already knew most of that stuff, by the way, so don't have a meltdown – and then said she needed to think about what she saw last night before calling her aunt," Michael replied.

Jack wasn't particularly surprised that Ivy confided about their unsettling evening to her father. "She said she needed to think?"

"Yes."

Things clicked into place for Jack. "I know exactly where she is."

"Where?"

"She's at the fairy ring … and I'm going to kill her."

IVY was lost in thought as she sat on the cold ground, her legs crossed and her palms resting on her knees. The weathered tree – which appeared to have a face – stared at her as she closed her eyes.

Ivy rolled her neck, releasing all negative thoughts just like Felicity taught her the first time she tried to meditate as a teenager. She focused inward instead of outward and then … jolted. A picture flashed through her mind, but it wasn't the one she expected. Instead she saw a vision of a woman sitting in a wooded field. It took her a moment to realize it was her, but the point of view seemed to indicate she was watching herself … from behind.

Ivy opened her eyes and jerked around, staring into the trees. Since it was fall, the leaves were missing from the branches and scattered about the carpeted forest. There were a few pine trees that afforded shelter and camouflage, including one that would offer cover to someone spying on her from the exact location as the vision suggested.

Ivy's heart hammered as she rolled to her feet, her eyes never leaving the tree. The sound of a branch snapping in that direction caused her stomach to twist. She had no idea what to do.

"Hello?"

It was a lame greeting, but her mind was blank when she tried to think of another option. The only thing coursing through her mind was getting away from the tree. She could run to her house – which was closer – but she would have to travel too close for comfort to that location if she picked that direction. The only other option was the nursery.

Ivy didn't give it another second of thought, turning to her right and bolting in that direction. This time she was sure she heard footsteps, but she didn't glance over her shoulder because she knew it would slow her down. She increased her pace, the blood rushing past her ears and drowning out everything else, and when she turned a corner she slammed into a wide chest.

She slapped out wildly, trying to step back and keep her balance at the same time. *How did he get ahead of me when he was coming from the other direction?* "Let me go!"

Jack wouldn't let her go, though. "It's me."

The words were welcome, but Ivy couldn't stop the tears when she realized she was safe. "Jack!"

Thirteen

"Good morning, Sunshine."

Max was all smiles when Jack opened the front door to Ivy's house the next morning. Jack couldn't muster the energy to match the grin so he pressed his finger to his lips instead.

"Are you telling me to be quiet, or that I'm number one in your heart?" Max quipped.

"Ivy is still asleep and if you wake her up I'm going to punch you," Jack warned.

The seriousness of the moody police officer's expression told Max it was probably prudent to take his antics down a notch. "What's going on? Your text just told me to get over here."

Jack backed up so he could glance down the hallway and focus on the bedroom. The door was firmly shut and Ivy was out of it when he left her in the warm bed so he could shower. He checked on her again upon exiting the bathroom, tucked her feet under the covers even though he knew she would poke them out again, and quietly left her with what he hoped were pleasant dreams. He wanted her to remain quiet and oblivious until he'd already left for work. Leaving Max to deal with her ire was much better than taking on the dragon himself.

"Ivy is … going through something," Jack said, choosing his words carefully.

"Oh, that time of the month?" Max nodded sagely. "Just give her some Midol PMS and a bar of chocolate. She'll thaw."

"Not *that*," Jack said, cuffing Max. "This is serious."

"It's hard to take you seriously when you're sneaking around in the dead of the morning," Max said, sitting in the overstuffed chair at the edge of the living room. "What's going on?"

Jack licked his lips. He decided to hold nothing back when relating the past couple of days to Max. He didn't want the man to be in the dark. He launched into the tale, keeping things as brief as possible, and when he was done he couldn't help but hate the impish grin on Max's face.

"You're just messing with me, aren't you?" Max glanced around the room, focusing on the ceiling corners. "Are you filming me so Ivy can put it up on Facebook or something?"

"I'm serious," Jack said, tugging on his limited patience. He was starting to regret calling Max for reinforcements. The last thing Ivy needed was someone making fun of her when she was struggling. "When I found her by the fairy ring yesterday, she was terrified. She thought someone was watching her."

"You said she had a vision where she was watching herself."

"Yeah, I know," Jack said. "She believes she somehow ... I don't know ... got into the killer's brain. That's what I managed to ascertain between the tears ... and then the inevitable silence, anyway."

"We have to be on a hidden camera show," Max said, swiveling his head as he searched the room. "You're totally messing with me."

"I am not messing with you and if you say that again I'm going to punch you," Jack hissed. "She's upset.

She thinks she's losing her mind. She's convinced someone was in those woods watching her. She thinks someone was following her and that's why she ran."

"What do you think?" Max asked, forcing himself to be serious. "Did you see anyone in the woods?"

"No, but I wasn't looking either," Jack replied. "I went out there searching for her and she just came … booking … around the corner and smacked right into me. Her heart was racing and she was flushed. I thought maybe she was sick again, but then I realized it was something else. She was legitimately terrified."

"No offense, but I know my sister better than you," Max said. "She wouldn't be terrified of a stranger in the woods. She would be far more likely to beat him up than run."

"She's not terrified of someone hurting her – although I would encourage a few more self-preservation thoughts where she's concerned," Jack said. "She's terrified that she's going crazy. How can you not understand that?"

The serious set of Jack's shoulders told Max the man was not embellishing the matter. He legitimately believed it. The realization had a sobering effect on him. "She's not crazy," he said after a beat. "Maybe she really is seeing things through the killer's eyes.

"You said she saw something the day she found Jeff Johnson's body," he continued. "What was it?"

"She just went someplace else for a few seconds," Jack explained. "She said that it wasn't a place, but she could hear someone saying he didn't want to die."

"Jeff?"

"That's what she thinks."

"So … what? Do you think she's psychic?" Max was beyond confused. "I'm not sure I believe in that stuff."

"I didn't believe in any of it before I met her," Jack said. "Then I started sharing dreams with her, and we could control our locations and interact with one another. That's not normal either. That doesn't mean it's not wonderful.

"I think she's gifted," he continued. "I think she's always been gifted and for some reason her abilities are just starting to show. I have no idea why. I have faith in her and believe she's going to figure this out. We just have to give her time."

"Okay," Max said. "What do you want me to do?"

"Watch her," Jack replied. "I don't want her alone and I have to work on the Johnson case. It's more important than ever now. The sooner we solve it, the sooner things go back to normal."

"You hope."

"Yes, I definitely hope that," Jack said. "I don't want her alone in case it happens again."

"You mean you don't want me alone in case I lose my mind in a public setting, right?"

Jack sucked in a breath when he heard Ivy's voice, shifting his gaze to the hallway and finding her watching them with a dark expression on her face. She was in fuzzy sleep pants and a T-shirt, her long hair standing up in a hundred different directions. She looked both beautiful and terrible at the same time.

"No, that's not what I said or meant," Jack said.

"Here it comes," Max whispered. "She's going to kill us both."

Jack ignored him. "Ivy, you said yourself that someone was in the woods with you yesterday," Jack said, choosing his words carefully. "That means someone is following you. Maybe he realizes you're somehow getting into his head."

"You don't believe that's what's happening, though." Ivy's voice was accusatory.

"I don't know what's happening and I refuse to put you at risk," Jack said, keeping his tone even. He was determined not to let her draw him into a fight. "You mean too much to me. I want you safe, and that means you're spending the day with Max."

"You're not the boss of me." Ivy crossed her arms over her chest, the tilt of her chin reflecting willful stubbornness. "I can take care of myself."

Jack's patience was about to hit a wall. "Is that why you were shaking and crying when I found you yesterday?"

"I ... ." Ivy's eyes clouded over. "I don't need a babysitter."

"Max is not a babysitter," Jack said. "Max is your willing slave and he's excited to help you with the greenhouse preparations."

"Thanks, man," Max deadpanned. "I love being volunteered for manual labor."

"You'll live," Jack shot back. "I want her safe no matter what. That's the most important thing to me."

"Don't worry, man. I'm on it."

Jack shifted his eyes to Ivy. "Will you please agree to spend the day with Max?"

"No."

"Please?"

Ivy was angry, but Jack appeared so desperate she couldn't add to his distress. "Fine. I'm still really mad at you, though."

"I guess that's going to be my cross to bear this afternoon," Jack said. "I can put up with that as long as I know you're safe."

"I'm really mad," Ivy threatened. "Like … you're going to have to rub my back for three hours straight tonight I'm so mad."

Jack's lips curled. "Done."

"Fine," Ivy said. "I'm going to be really mean to Max, though."

"I think that's fair," Jack said, pressing his lips together as she stalked down the hallway. He didn't move until she slammed the bedroom door. "Don't let her out of your sight, Max. Something is going on here. Until we figure out what it is, I don't want her left alone."

"I'm not going to leave her alone, but when she's mean to me – and we both know that wasn't an idle threat – I'm going to take it out on you," Max said.

"I would rather face your wrath than hers," Jack said. "She's much more frightening."

"Isn't that the truth," Max muttered. "Did you see that hair?"

Jack smiled. "I happen to like the hair."

"You are one whipped man."

"And somehow I'm fine with that," Jack said. "I'm trusting you, Max. Don't let her bully you into walking away. This is important."

"Yeah, yeah. I've got it. Now … go. I'll take care of the Midwest's wickedest witch."

"Make sure you do."

"YOU NEED to give Jack a break."

Max spent the better part of the morning trying to appeal to Ivy's reasonable side. When he realized it wouldn't be visiting his sister's home today, he decided to play on her sympathy.

"I don't need to do anything," Ivy countered.

"He's worried about you," Max said. "That's allowed because he's in love with you and he's already at that place where he hurts when you hurt … or he freaks out when you freak out … or he believes in magic when you believe in magic."

Ivy elbowed Max's stomach as she moved in front of him and hit the trail that led from her house to the nursery. She cast a forlorn look in the direction of her fairy ring – which was out of sight but at the forefront of her brain – as she passed.

"I wish he wouldn't have told you any of that," Ivy grumbled. "It wasn't his place."

"I'm your brother."

"I don't care."

"I love you, too," Max said. "You don't have to hide things from me. I may tease you, but when it comes down to it, I'll always have your back. You know that, right?"

Ivy sighed as she ran her finger over the tender spot between her eyebrows. "I love you, too. You're a pain in the butt, though."

"I know."

"I think you might be a mental midget, too."

"It's not nice to use the 'M' word."

"Midget?" Ivy wrinkled her nose. "Since when is that a bad word?"

"I was talking about mental," Max said. "You're the one who thinks you were looking through a killer's eyes. I think that makes you mental."

"I want to kick you."

"I might let you if … ." Max broke off and stared into the woods, uncertain. "Let's go to the fairy ring."

Ivy balked. "What? Why?"

"Because I want you to show me exactly where you think someone was watching you from," Max replied. "We might be able to spot footprints or something. Did Jack look?"

"No. He was more interested in getting me back to the nursery … and then hovering for the entire afternoon. He wouldn't leave my side and I didn't want to go back to the clearing."

"Are you afraid to go there now?"

Ivy took the question as a challenge. "I'm not afraid of anything."

"We both know that's not true," Max said. "You're afraid of my mental superiority … and you're not hugely fond of spiders."

Ivy snorted and made an exaggerated face.

"You're also afraid of my manliness and the fact that I'll put your head in my armpit if you're not careful," Max threatened.

Ivy blew out a sigh. He always knew exactly which buttons to push. "Fine. Lead the way. If someone is out there, though, I'm totally running. It's going to be up to you to keep up."

"Don't worry," Max said, slinging an arm over her shoulders as they headed into the trees. "I'll protect you, dear sister."

"Somehow I think I'm going to be the one protecting you if we're attacked," Ivy muttered.

It took the duo five minutes to reach the fairy ring, and when they did, Ivy instinctively drew closer to her brother. Max noticed the movement but didn't comment. Internally he was upset, though. This was Ivy's favorite place. He was angry anyone would dare attempt to ruin it for her.

"Where were you?" Max asked.

Ivy pointed to the spot right in front of the tree. "There."

"Okay. Go and sit exactly how you were sitting."

Ivy didn't look thrilled with the prospect. "Max … ."

"It will be fine. I promise."

Ivy scuffed her boots against the fallen leaves as she trudged to the location and lowered herself to the ground. She refused to turn her back in case Max was attacked – or if something else happened – and watched as Max moved closer to the pine tree.

"Is this the tree?" Max asked.

"Yeah. I heard a branch snap … after."

"Okay." Max moved to the side of the tree and peered behind it. He briefly considered pretending someone was grabbing his arm, but he didn't think Ivy's frazzled nerves could take the joke so he opted to play it straight instead. "The leaves are disturbed back here."

"They are?" Ivy didn't know if she was relieved or more worried by the admission.

"That doesn't mean it was a person," Max reminded her. "It could've been an animal."

"But it wasn't."

"Can you see me?" Max disappeared behind the tree.

"No. Can you see me?"

"Yeah. I have a clear view through the branches," Max replied. "Someone definitely could've spied on you from here. When you started running toward the nursery, what did you hear?"

"Footsteps."

"Are you sure?"

"I'm sure."

"Well, I hate to say it, but it does look like someone ran through here," Max said, appearing on the other side of the tree. "I'm starting to lean toward the 'you're not crazy' theory. Congratulations!"

"Ha, ha," Ivy intoned, getting to her feet. "Do you think it was a man or a woman?"

"I'm not a Native American scout, so I have no idea," Max said. "I do think someone was out here, though."

"So … what do we do?"

"We go to the greenhouse and call Jack," Max answered. "We tell him what we found and then let him deal with the repercussions."

"I don't want to call Jack," Ivy complained, falling into step with Max. "He's on my butthead list right now."

"Oh, how cute," Max said, tweaking Ivy's nose. "You're going to punish him later, aren't you?"

"You have no idea."

"If your mind just went to a filthy place, I don't want to hear it," Max said. "You've turned into a real pervert since you started dating Jack."

"And you've turned into a pain in the butt since the day you were born."

"Oh, such a lame comeback."

Max and Ivy kept up the verbal sparring until they reached the nursery, and despite herself, Ivy felt better. Max knew exactly how to brighten her spirits – by being a moron – and she was almost ready to let go of her anger when she noticed the door to the greenhouse was open.

"What the … ?"

"Did you leave it like that?" Max asked, confused.

"I never leave it like that," Ivy said. "Someone must've been in here. If Dad messed up my decorations, he's going to be in big trouble."

Max instinctively reached out and grabbed Ivy's arm before she could touch the door handle. He yanked her back to the spot in front of him and glanced around, as if searching for a specific face.

"What are you doing?" Ivy asked.

"That door was jimmied, Ivy," Max said, pointing toward the grooves on the wood next to the lock. "That means someone broke in. Dad didn't do this."

Grim realization caused Ivy's shoulders to sink. "Do you think … ?"

She didn't finish the question because Max was already pulling his phone out of his pocket. "I don't know what to think," he said. "I'm definitely calling Jack, though."

Fourteen

"What do you have?"

Brian and Jack arrived at the nursery ten minutes after Max called. Brian couldn't be sure, but it was almost as if Jack was expecting the eldest Morgan sibling to have an emergency. Jack was morose from the moment he hit the station, and then he proceeded to fixate on his files and investigation notes instead of engaging in menial chitchat. Brian was alert from the beginning of his shift. Then, when the call came, Jack practically bolted through the door.

"We came up to the greenhouse from that direction," Max said, pointing toward the woods on the other side of the structure. "We noticed the door was open right away. At first Ivy thought Dad might've gone in there, but then I caught sight of the grooves."

"I see them," Brian said, hunkering down so he could study the tool marks on an even level. "I think someone used the claw side of a hammer to push it open. Have you been inside?"

"We thought it was better to wait for you," Max said.

"That's smart," Jack said, shifting his eyes to a belligerent-looking Ivy. She stood next to the naked maple at the edge of the building, her arms crossed over her chest, and glared daggers in his direction. "Are you okay?"

"I'm mad at you."

"That's not what I asked," Jack prodded. "Are you okay?"

"She's fine," Max said. "She's just … being her."

"Yes, well, I would appreciate hearing the words from her," Jack said. "I'm not asking you to give up your anger. I am asking for some common decency when I ask you a pointed question."

Ivy extended her tongue and blew out a loud and wet sigh. "I'm fine."

"Great," Jack said, earning a curious look from Brian. "What?"

"What happened to the flowers and unicorns you two usually toss at one another when you're in close proximity?" the older cop asked. "Trouble in paradise?"

"We're fighting," Jack replied. "She's entitled to her anger. Although … I would like to point out that this little incident actually proves I was right to call Max to hang out with you today."

"Ah, I understand now," Brian said, shaking his head. "You went into protection mode and she's got her hackles up. She'll get over it."

"I know," Jack said, turning back to the door. "Let's check out the inside and see if anything has been messed with."

"I think you're going to need me for that," Ivy called out. "I'm the only one who knows if something has been touched."

"I'm going to touch you with my foot in your behind if you're not careful," Jack threatened, pushing open the door. "I was just here the other night. I know exactly how it's supposed to look."

Jack took a bold step inside and frowned. "Huh."

"What?" Brian asked, moving to his side. "Do you see something?"

Jack swiveled, his eyes busy as they took in all the work Ivy had done. He'd been in the greenhouse the day before, but he didn't give it a good look before tearing off into the woods after Ivy. Once they returned he was too distracted to pay attention.

"I have no idea if anything has been touched," Jack admitted. "It looks like one great big mess to me."

Brian pursed his lips together to keep from laughing as he cast his gaze toward the open door. "Ivy, do you want to take a look around?"

Ivy was haughty as she sauntered inside, Max close on her heels. She moved through the greenhouse methodically, scanning every nook and cranny. When she got close to Jack, she made a big show of stepping around his tense body without touching him. One look at his partner told Brian this was pure torture for the man.

"Anything?" Brian asked after a few minutes.

"I don't think anything is missing," Ivy said. "Those pots weren't there yesterday, though." She pointed to three clay pots with painted faces on a nearby shelf. "They were on the ground."

"Okay, well, we're going to see if we can process this place for fingerprints," Brian said. "We'll focus on the door and the pots."

"That won't ruin anything, will it?" Ivy's expression slipped. "I've put so much work into the greenhouse."

Jack took pity on her. "I won't let them ruin anything."

"I'm still mad at you," Ivy muttered.

"I still won't let them ruin anything," Jack said. "I mean ... if you give me a hug, I won't let them ruin anything."

"No way!" Ivy stomped her foot against the ground. "That's not how being angry works. I can't give you a hug when I'm ticked off because you're being a jackhole."

Jack extended a threatening finger. "I've told you numerous times not to call me that," he said. "I don't like you using my name as an insult."

"I've been using that word since I was a kid!"

"She has," Max confirmed. "It's not a new thing. It's bad luck for you, but it's hardly because of you."

"Thank you, Max," Jack intoned. "What else have you been doing today … besides ganging up on me, I mean?"

"We went to the fairy ring."

Jack's temper flared at the words. "You took her to the fairy ring after what happened?"

"What happened?" Brian asked, curiosity getting the better of him.

"Nothing." Jack, Ivy, and Max answered in unison.

"Something obviously happened," Brian argued.

"How about you just call for the tech team and I'll handle this conversation?" Jack suggested, his tone sugary sweet even though the words had some kick.

"Fine." Brian held up his hands. "I'm too old for this drama anyway. I'll be outside."

"Thanks."

Jack waited until he was sure Brian was out of earshot before he exploded. "How could you take her out there? What if something had happened to her?"

"I wanted to see it for myself," Max replied, unruffled. "Someone was definitely standing behind that tree and I swear it looked as if someone was running through the leaves. They were all messed up."

"Really?" Jack was both agitated and relieved by the news.

"Oh, see, he thought I was crazy and now he can breathe easier because I wasn't making it up," Ivy complained.

"I never thought you were making it up," Jack snapped. "I … ." He had no idea how he was supposed to fix the problem so he switched tactics. "Hopefully we'll find some prints and track down whoever is doing this. It won't be long now."

Ivy snorted. "You don't know that," she said. "What if whoever broke in here doesn't have prints on file? What if whoever broke in here isn't the same person who killed Jeff Johnson? What if … ?"

Jack closed the distance between them and shut her up with a scorching kiss before she could get a full head of steam. When he took a step back, they were both red-faced and gasping.

"Why did you do that?"

"Because I needed to kiss you," Jack answered. "You can go back to being mad now."

"I … ." Ivy looked helpless. "Beat him up, Max! That was uncalled for."

"Oh, no," Max intoned. "I'm staying out of this freak show. There's no way I'm getting involved. You people are on your own."

"DO YOU want to tell me what's up with you and Ivy?"

After the state police's tech team left Ivy's greenhouse – and Max and Jack worked overtime to fix the door so no one else could wander inside – the two police officers returned to the station. Jack refused to talk about the incident at the greenhouse all afternoon, and by the time Jeff Johnson's visitation rolled around, Brian was pretty much at his wit's end.

They walked to the funeral parlor in silence, but five minutes of watching Jack scan the room from a corner was pretty much all Brian could take.

"Nothing is up with Ivy and me," Jack replied. "We're just … fighting. We always fight. You should recognize the act."

"You don't usually fight like this, though."

"Sure we do."

"No, you usually fight in a way that makes it clear you're going to rip each other's clothes off the minute you get home," Brian said. "Now, that makes me uncomfortable because I've known her since she was knee-high and running around in pigtails. I pretend not to notice, though.

"What I saw this afternoon was completely different, my friend," he continued. "She's clearly angry and you're letting her maintain distance because … well, I'm not rightly sure why you're letting her do it."

"It's a private thing."

"Since when is anything you do with Ivy private?" Brian challenged. "I've spent months listening to talk about her eyes … and smile … and the cute way she snores when she's really tired. If you wanted to enact privacy rules, you should've done it before I had to listen to that."

"It's not something I can really talk about," Jack said. "Basically I called Max to watch her today because I'm not convinced her illness is really behind her and she's ticked off." It wasn't exactly a lie. It wasn't the complete truth either.

"Oh, is that all?" Brian furrowed his brow. "She'll get over that."

"I hope so," Jack said, shifting his eyes to the door and groaning when he saw Ivy and Max walk through it. "Seriously? Is she trying to kill me?"

Brian pressed his lips together to keep from laughing at Jack's outraged expression. Personally, he wasn't at all surprised to see Ivy. She was just as involved in the case as his partner. The fact that Jack somehow believed she would actually remain behind was almost cute, though.

"Don't go over there," Brian warned, grabbing Jack's arm and jerking him back toward the corner when the taller man made a move to intercept Ivy. "She's not doing anything wrong and she knew Jeff for a number of years. She has a right to pay her respects."

"She's supposed to be home," Jack gritted out. "She's supposed to be resting."

"And you're supposed to be focusing on the potential suspects in this room," Brian pointed out. "Who do you think has a motive?"

"They all seem to have a convoluted motive if you want to break it down in that manner," Jack said, briefly locking gazes with Ivy and scowling when she feigned happiness and offered him an exaggerated wave. "I'm going to ... ."

"You're going to blow your stack and then beg her to forgive you because the nights are getting cold and you're addicted to her pie," Brian said, realizing the double meaning of what he said when it was too late to take it back. "Er, wait. That might've come out wrong."

"Oh, pie," Jack complained. "She was going to make me an apple pie before I ticked her off. Well, I'll never see that."

"You'll see it. Stop being so dramatic."

"I can't help myself," Jack admitted. "She makes me nuts."

"You make her nuts, too. That's why you work."

"I'm not sure I can take much more of this, though," Jack said, gesturing in Ivy's direction as she moved to Karen's side. "She's pretending I'm not even in the room."

"She's doing that for your benefit because she wants you to break first," Brian supplied. "It's a power struggle. If you go over there, she wins. If she comes over here, you win."

"In what scenario do we both win?"

"The one where you go home together and pretend nothing happened once you're out of the public eye."

"I hope that happens soon," Jack said, shaking himself out of his reverie and turning his attention to the door. "I ... uh-oh."

"I don't like the sound of that," Brian said, following his partner's gaze. "What do you see?"

Jack pointed toward the doorframe between the lobby and the viewing room and shook his head when Maisie Washington strode through the archway. She was decked out in a short black dress with fishnet stockings and one of those pill hats with a little veil. She looked like a grieving widow, not a furious mistress.

"Oh, well, this isn't going to go well," Jack said, moving to intercept Maisie. It was already too late, though. She'd caught sight of Karen and was heading in that direction.

"You!" Maisie planted her hands on her hips and stared Karen down. "You killed him, didn't you? You knew we were going to be happy and you just couldn't stand losing to the better woman."

"Can someone throw out the trash?" Karen asked, lazily running her hand over her huge belly. She didn't even make a move to get out of the chair.

"I'm talking to you!" Maisie moved to grab Karen's arm, but Ivy stopped her with a slap of the hand. Maisie's eyes widened. "Are you seriously getting involved in this?"

"Don't push me," Ivy warned. "I've already proven I'll take you down just because I enjoy it. If you touch Karen again, though, I'm going to do it in front of all these people."

"Son of a … ." Jack muttered under his breath as he shot Ivy a warning look. She steadfastly ignored him.

"You're not a part of this," Maisie snapped.

"Neither are you," Karen pointed out. "Jeff was still my husband. You're nothing here. You're not even that filmy crust left over the next morning after people cry themselves to sleep. I want you out of here."

"I have every right to be here," Maisie argued. "I was the love of Jeff's life."

"If that's true, how come he didn't leave Karen?" Ivy challenged. "If you guys were going to live happily ever after, how come he didn't take the first step and make you happy?"

"I … ." Maisie's mouth dropped open. "You don't know what you're talking about. Mind your own business!"

"Okay, Maisie, I think that's enough," Brian said, grabbing her arm. "It's not your place to do this. You shouldn't be making a scene. Show some respect."

"Respect? Have they been respecting me?"

"What's to respect?" Ivy asked. "You're a whore. You've always been a whore."

"Ivy!" Jack was dumbfounded by her response. He knew she didn't like Maisie, but she was downright aggressive whenever the woman showed her face these days. "I think you should leave, too."

"Oh, don't worry about it," Karen said, struggling to her feet. "I'm pretty sure I'm the one who is going to leave. I can't take one more minute of this ... tripe."

For one brief moment Karen looked as if she was stable ... and then she pitched forward. Only Jack's reflexes stopped her from crashing into the glass coffee table in front of the couch.

"Call the paramedics," Jack bellowed, struggling to maintain Karen's weight. "Tell them there's a pregnant woman in distress. Someone call them right now."

Fifteen

"How is she?"

Ivy spent the first twenty minutes after her arrival at the clinic pacing the lobby without making eye contact with Jack. Once she saw Dr. Nesbitt call him and Brian into a room to brief them on Karen's prognosis, she tried to listen outside the door, but Jack shut it so she couldn't hear – which offended her and elated him when he saw her furious face through the window. Finally she had no choice but to approach him – which was exactly what he wanted.

"I'm not sure I'm supposed to share private medical information with you," Jack said, crossing his arms as he leaned against the wall. "That's against procedure … and with you being mad and all … well, you know."

"Are you sure this is the hill you want to die on, son?" Brian asked.

Jack ignored him as Ivy scowled.

"That's just mean," Ivy said finally. "I'm not asking you to give me down and dirty details. I'm asking if she's going to be okay. Nothing more."

Jack was taken aback by her attitude. "She's going to be fine. She was just dehydrated."

"Great," Ivy said, blowing out a heavy breath and glancing toward the closed hospital room door. "Is she staying overnight? Does she need anything?"

"Her parents are handling that," Brian said. "She's not accepting visitors … so you might as well go home."

"Um … okay." Ivy scuffed her foot against the floor as she trudged toward the door.

Jack watched her, a mixture of amusement, irritation, and adoration flitting across his face when he was sure she wasn't looking, but his smile slipped when something occurred to him. "Where is Max?"

"Max? He's … um … otherwise engaged."

"What does that mean, Ivy?"

"It's the barn's annual holiday beer night."

"Was that supposed to be an answer or something?" Jack asked his partner, confused.

"It's kind of a Halloween singles mixer," Brian explained. "All the young people who are hot to trot and unattached get dressed up in costumes and attend the barn's beer night."

"And Max just abandoned you in town to go there?" Jack was annoyed.

"He didn't want to stay and I told him he could go because he was desperate not to miss this year's honeys. It's really my fault."

"Uh-huh." Jack had no idea what he was going to do, and when he spoke again, even he was surprised by what slipped out. "Oh, well, that's too bad. Now you're going to have to walk home."

Brian's mouth dropped open, stunned disbelief coursing through him. Jack was usually the first one to acquiesce to all of Ivy's pouty moods. He held his ground this time, though. It was mighty impressive.

"Fine." Ivy was stubborn in her own right. If Jack thought the threat of a cold-weather walk was enough to cause her to give in, he was sadly mistaken. She would wade through a foot of snow before admitting defeat. "I guess I'll … see you around, huh?"

Jack's heart twisted at the words even as his temper flared. "I guess so."

Ivy pressed her lips together and nodded, faking a smile for Brian before heading toward the door. "Have a nice night."

"You, too."

Jack maintained his composure until she was out the door and heading for the sidewalk. Then he kicked one of the metal lobby chairs and sent it careening across the room.

"That woman is the most stubborn creature on the planet!"

"Calm down," Brian chided. "It's not as if you were on your best behavior either."

"I did not create this situation and you're the one who told me I had to be strong if I didn't want her to gain all of the power in the relationship. I was just following your advice."

"Huh. I did say that, didn't I?" Brian rubbed the back of his neck. "I've been known to be wrong a time or two."

"I knew it," Jack muttered, striding toward the door. "Now I'm going to have to beg her to forgive me. This is all your fault!"

"Just pick her up," Brian suggested. "It's cold tonight and she's wearing a light coat and open-toed shoes. She's going to be frozen by the time you get to her."

The reality of Brian's words caused Jack's heart to flip. "Now I'm really mad at you. You know that, right?"

Brian shrugged. "I don't care if you have to walk home in the dark. She's a different story. There's a murderer out there, in case you've forgotten."

Jack wanted to throw up. "Son of a ... !"

"GET IN the truck."

Jack drove five miles an hour down Main Street, his head poking out the open window of his truck as Ivy stomped along the sidewalk a few feet away. The downtown was mostly abandoned, but they still got the occasional stare from passersby.

"Oh, no. I'm walking. That's what you want, isn't it?"

"No, that's not even remotely what I want."

'That's not what you said."

"Get in the truck, Ivy," Jack snapped, averting his gaze as Henry Higgins, the owner of the local bookstore, looked up from the walk he was sweeping and watched the show. "It's freezing and you're still getting over being sick."

"You didn't care about that ten minutes ago."

If Jack thought she was stubborn before, she was downright mulish now. She was digging her heels in and he was going to have no choice but to grovel. He just knew it.

"Do you want me to leave you here?" It was Jack's last-ditch effort to get her to come to him. "Is that what you want?"

"I … ." Ivy shifted her eyes to the trees on the other side of the street and frowned. Ever since the previous day, she couldn't shake the feeling of being watched … and she didn't like it. The idea of walking past those trees by herself was daunting … and that was on top of the steadily dropping temperature.

Jack recognized the fear on her face and hated himself for making her go through it. "Honey, please get in the truck," he pleaded, adjusting his tone. "I'm sorry. I don't want to fight. I want to take you home and make sure you're warm."

"And then what?"

"I ... don't know."

Ivy pressed the heel of her hand against her cheek, uncertain. "I don't want you to take me home and then leave."

Jack was surprised by the admission, but he was pretty sure it was the closest he was going to get to a compromise tonight. "I'm not leaving. Depending on how mean you are, I might sleep on the couch, but I won't leave you."

Ivy licked her lips and nodded as she headed to the truck. She wordlessly opened the door and hoisted herself inside, fastening the seatbelt before she spoke again. "I don't want you to sleep on the couch either."

"We still have a few things to talk about," Jack warned.

"I don't care. I ... ."

"It's okay," Jack said, reaching over to capture her hand and finding it ice cold. "Oh, you're freezing." He turned up the heat and moved her hands in front of the vent. "I'll start a fire when we get to your house."

"Can we cuddle under a blanket while we fight?"

Jack weighed the question from both sides. "Absolutely," he said finally, cracking a grin. "You have hot chocolate and cookies, too, right?"

Ivy nodded.

"What about my pie?"

"We'll see how the night goes."

"GIVE ME your feet."

Jack stoked the flames until the room was practically roasting and then placed a blanket on the floor in front of the stone fireplace and motioned for Ivy to join him.

"What do you mean?" Ivy was puzzled.

"You were out walking in the cold in open-toed shoes, and I'm going to make sure your feet are warm," Jack said. "You lose most of your body heat through your head and feet. Both of yours were uncovered."

"This seems silly, but I'm not in the mood for even more fighting, so ... whatever." Ivy sat on the blanket and watched as Jack tugged off her shoes and wrapped his hands around her bare toes. He seemed focused on his task, but also distracted. "Can I ask you a question, Jack?"

He shifted his eyes to her. "I guess."

"Do you ever think I'm so much work I'm not worth it?"

The question was earnest and it tugged at Jack's heartstrings. "No."

"Never?"

"Not for one second of one day," Jack replied. "That doesn't mean you're perfect, or that your attitude today was something to applaud. You purposely made things more difficult for me, and I don't appreciate that."

Ivy pressed her lips together as Jack finished rubbing her feet. He grabbed another blanket off the couch and settled behind her, placing the blanket over both of them and pulling her back against his chest as he rested against the couch.

"I didn't set out this morning with the express goal of making things more difficult for you," Ivy said, adopting a diplomatic tone. "That wasn't my aim."

"I almost believe that," Jack said. "The problem is, I think I encouraged you a little this morning and you were originally treating it like a game. We both do that sometimes. It came back to bite us today."

"Yes, but I didn't do it on purpose."

"I know you didn't, Ivy, but you need to cut me some slack right now," Jack said. He was serious and straightforward. "There is a murderer running around Shadow Lake, and it looks like he's interested in you. Do you want to know how I know that? You've seen it with your own eyes."

"What if I haven't, though?" Her voice was so tiny Jack had to strain to hear her.

"And I think that's what's really bothering you and I didn't reassure you enough on that front this morning," Jack surmised. "You're not going crazy, honey. You're not imagining it. I think that deep down you already know that. On the surface, though, you're less sure."

"I don't know what to think," Ivy admitted. "It's like my worst nightmare from childhood is coming true."

"What do you mean?" Jack pushed Ivy's hair behind her ear so he could rub his cheek against hers. Despite her limited time outside, she was still cold and he was only too happy to warm her up.

"Everyone called me strange and weird when I was a kid," Ivy said. "I wasn't invited to any of the parties … and no one wanted to sit next to me in class. I eventually got used to it, but if people find out about this … ."

"Honey, no one is going to find out about it," Jack said. "Even if they do, though, it doesn't matter. I'm always going to invite you to my parties and I'm always going to want to sit next to you in class. I don't care what anyone else thinks."

Ivy reluctantly giggled. "Sometimes I think I'm the luckiest woman in the world because I found you."

"I know you're the luckiest woman in the world," Jack said. "I know I'm the luckiest man in the world, too. Whatever this is, Ivy, we're going to figure it out. It's going to be okay."

"Unless I really am crazy."

"You're not crazy," Jack snapped, tilting her chin with his finger so she had no choice but to look at him. "I have nothing but faith in you. You're a total pain in the butt when you want to be. You're often rude and crude. You're still the best person I know … and you are magical.

"Don't let this wear you down," he continued. "Max said someone was out in the woods watching you. That's validation for what you said happened. I didn't need that validation, though, because I already believed you.

"Now, as for your fight with Maisie at the funeral home, you seriously need to back off from her," he said. "She's a crazy woman, but you're not doing yourself any favors when it comes to smarting off to her."

"I don't know why I did that," Ivy said. "Sometimes I think my mouth has a mind of its own."

Jack smirked. "Oh, yeah? What does your mouth's mind want to do right now?"

Ivy sucked in her cheeks to hide her smile. "Well, I have a few ideas."

"One of them better involve cookies."

"Oh, I was going to bake a pie for you," Ivy said, grinning when he tickled her ribs.

"It's too late to bake a pie, although I'm not ruling it out for later this week," Jack said. "I just want cookies … and you out of this skirt."

"Oh, I do declare, that is just untoward."

Jack loved the cutesy accent. "You can punish me later for my filthy mouth, ma'am."

Ivy sobered. "No more punishment tonight for either of us. I can't take it."

"Deal."

Jack lowered his mouth to hers and gave her a sweet kiss. "Now take off that skirt while I grab the cookies."

"Yes, sir."

"Do you want hot chocolate, too?"

"Did you just meet me?"

"Two mugs of hot chocolate coming up," Jack said, hopping to his feet. "Pick a movie on cable. I would prefer we stay away from the chick flicks."

Ivy made a face. "Chick flicks? It's Halloween season. We have to watch a horror movie."

"I think our lives are filled with enough horror right now."

"But ... it's *The Shining*," Ivy whined, pointing toward the television screen as she clicked to AMC. "It's just starting, too."

"Fine," Jack conceded. "If you have a nightmare, though, don't come crying to me."

"Really?"

"No," Jack said, shaking his head. "If you have a nightmare, I don't want you crying to anyone else but me."

"That was a much better answer."

"Just wait until I do my imitation of that kid and his imaginary friend," Jack warned. "Red rum. Red rum. Red rum."

Ivy barked out a laugh. "This turned out to be a good night after all, huh?"

"Every night with you is the best night, honey," Jack said. "Now ... take off your skirt. Don't make me ask you again."

"You're so bossy."

"And don't you forget it."

Sixteen

"What is all of this?"

Jack wandered into the kitchen the next morning and his eyes practically bugged out of his head when he saw the feast on the table. Ivy showered first and seemed to be in good spirits when she left him in the bathroom. He had no idea she planned on filling him full of good food before he left for the day, and the realization when he saw all of her hard work on his behalf warmed him. She had a sweet side she didn't want anyone but him to see. It made him feel special … and incredibly hungry.

"It's omelets, hash browns, and toast," Ivy replied. "I also poured you juice and coffee."

Jack arched a bewildered eyebrow. "Am I dying?"

"Ha, ha," Ivy intoned, making a face. "It's not funny when you say that. You didn't like it when I said it."

"Yeah, but I said it as a joke," Jack said, kissing her cheek before sitting at the table. "You said it when you were burning up in my arms."

"Well, I still don't like it," Ivy said, taking her seat. "I just wanted to cook something nice for you after I was such a pain yesterday."

"I like it when you're a pain."

"You didn't like it yesterday."

"That was mostly because Brian told me if I apologized to you and begged for forgiveness I was handing over all of the power in the relationship," Jack said. "The way he made it sound, that was bad."

Ivy made a face. "I think I'm going to have a talk with Brian."

"Leave it alone," Jack said. "He was laughing at me when you stormed out of the funeral home and admitted he might occasionally be wrong."

"He was definitely wrong yesterday," Ivy said. "Still … I'm sorry."

Jack knew how hard it was for her to admit that. "I'm sorry, too. I'm not sorry for worrying about you and trying to keep you safe, but I am sorry for upsetting you. I don't like doing that."

"Well, that makes two of us." Ivy's smile was back in place until she saw her front door open – with no accompanying knock – to allow Max entry. He looked bright-eyed and shiny, and Ivy knew exactly what that meant. "You got lucky with one of your honeys, didn't you?"

Jack smirked as Max sat at the table and grabbed a slice of toast from Ivy's plate.

"A gentleman never reveals the nature of his night," Max replied. "I am not a gentleman, though. I totally got lucky."

"You almost didn't get lucky with me," Jack countered. "Is there a reason you left Ivy alone at the clinic?"

Max balked. "She said she was going home with you."

"Really?" Jack's expression was thoughtful as his eyes drifted to Ivy. "That's not what you said last night."

Ivy shifted on her chair, averting her gaze. "Oh, um … ."

"You wanted to make up and you forced a situation where we would have no choice, didn't you?" Jack couldn't help but smile. "That is so manipulative."

"It worked like a charm too," Ivy pointed out.

"I'll bet you didn't think that when you were walking home alone," Jack argued. "As for leaving her, Max, next time please check with me. I would've told you to go, too. I was just as sick of the fight as she was. I still don't want to risk her being alone right now."

"Why do you think I'm here?" Max asked, using a fork to cut into Jack's omelet so he could take a big bite. "I figured I was on Ivy duty again today."

"I wouldn't call it that if I were you," Jack said. "I would appreciate you spending the day with Ivy, though."

"You know I can hear you two talking, right?" Ivy challenged.

The two men ignored her.

"It's fine," Max said. "It's a slow time of year for the lumber yard. I would love to spend some quality time with my sister."

"Good deal." Jack was pleased with Max's words but not the food theft. "That's my omelet."

"I'm hungry, though," Max complained.

"There's another omelet for you being kept warm in the oven," Ivy supplied. "I knew you would be here because Jack is nothing if not predictable."

"That's not what you said last night," Jack shot back.

"Don't make me kill you," Max warned, retrieving his breakfast. "That's still my sister."

"You'll live," Jack said. "Are you really telling me you're not going to put up a fight about having to stick close to Max?" Jack was understandably dubious.

"I'm really telling you that," Ivy confirmed. "The haunted greenhouse opens tomorrow. I have a lot of work to finish today. Max is going to be very busy doing my bidding."

"Well, that sounds like a plan," Jack said. "If something happens, though … ." He left the rest of the statement hanging.

"I'll call you," Ivy said. "I promise."

"Call me whether something happens or not," Jack said. "I have a feeling I might miss you if you don't."

"Ugh." Max slammed his breakfast plate down on the table. "You two make my stomach churn." That didn't stop him from forking a huge heap of hash browns into his mouth.

"Something tells me you'll survive," Jack said dryly.

"YOU AND Jack seem better," Max said, trailing behind Ivy as they headed toward the greenhouse an hour later. "Did you kiss and make up?"

"We were mean to each other for a little bit, then we were nice, and then we made up," Ivy replied, smiling at the memory. "We watched *The Shining*. There might've been a few kisses."

"You're so gooey this morning I want to rub your face in my armpit just to bring you back to reality."

"If you do that, I'll make you cry," Ivy warned.

"As long as you're not crying, I think it's going to be a good day," Max said. "Did anything happen at the hospital after I left you?"

Ivy shook her head. "Dr. Nesbitt said it was just dehydration, but I can't imagine all of this stress is good for Karen. She's so close to having the baby. It would be a tragedy if something went wrong now."

"Can't they … I don't know … take the baby early?" Max asked.

"It's not like a pitch … or carrots, for that matter," Ivy replied. "It's best if a baby comes when it's supposed to come. I just feel so bad for Karen. I can't believe Maisie did that."

"Really?" Max made a hilarious face as he struck a very Maisie-like pose. "The world is all about Maisie. How can you not know that?"

Ivy giggled. "She has a lot of balls to show up at the funeral home like that, though," she said. "Everyone already knows she was having an affair with Jeff. Why would she possibly want to rub it in Karen's face the way she did? It just makes her look bad."

"Maisie is one of those chicks who can't see what's right in front of her," Max said. "She thinks everything is about her. She's too narcissistic to think that anyone else has feelings."

"Well, it was still wrong," Ivy said. "I have half a mind to go to the library and beat her up."

Max snorted. "You're pretty feisty where Maisie is concerned these days. I know you've never liked her, but you're especially irritated when she's in a room now. What gives?"

Ivy shrugged. "I honestly have no idea," she said. "I can't seem to stop myself from seeing red when she's around. Like … literally seeing red. Whenever she opens her mouth I want to shove my fist in it to silence her."

"Wow," Max intoned. "That was almost violently poetic."

"I should be a writer," Ivy said, smiling as she reached for the greenhouse door. "Still, don't you think it's weird that Maisie would risk the wrath of two grieving families to make a scene? It's not as if she's going to get anything out of it."

"I don't think Maisie is the type of person who strategically plans out her life," Max said, following Ivy into the greenhouse. He gave the room a good once-over before continuing, but nothing looked out of place. "Take you, for example. I can tell you're trying to figure out the best way to tell Jack you love him.

"Don't bother denying it," he continued, touching his fingertip to his sister's burning cheek. "I'm your big brother. I know everything you're thinking."

"You don't know crap," Ivy groused, jerking her face away from his hand. "Don't touch me. You'll make my face dirty."

Max ignored the admonishment. "I know that you want to tell Jack you love him but you're afraid he won't say it back to you," he said. "He will."

"You don't know that."

"I know it," Max said. "When he first showed up in our lives, I didn't like him. I'm not going to lie. I thought he was weird and I couldn't figure out why he looked at you the way he did.

"At first I thought he suspected you were a murderer or something," he continued. "Then I thought he wanted to lock you up for being crazy. It took me a little bit of time to realize that all of those looks meant he was completely enamored with you. You stole his heart, Ivy. He wasn't expecting it either.

"Now, I like Jack a great deal," he said. "He's good for you and I've never seen you this happy. I want this to work out – and not just because Jack would be some formidable opposition on the singles circuit. I want you to be happy, Ivy. To do that, you've got to let go of the fear."

They were nice words, but Ivy still wasn't convinced. "If you're so sure he loves me, why hasn't he said it?"

"Because he's as nervous as you are," Max replied. "He's afraid you won't say it back."

"That's ridiculous."

"Is it?" Max challenged. "You two fell hard and fast for each other. You're still feeling your way around. There's no reason to push things."

"I want to push you," Ivy muttered. "I might even push you over a cliff."

"Promises, promises," Max teased, turning to the business at hand. "Where do you want me to start?"

TWO HOURS later the greenhouse was almost completely put together and Ivy's spirits were high. The more she thought about Max's words regarding Jack's feelings, the more she believed he was right. Of course, she rationalized that could also be wishful thinking.

Ivy was so lost in thought, she didn't realize her mind was wandering until she leaned her head against the counter and a picture drifted to the forefront of her brain. As if in a trance, Ivy watched the scene play out as her stomach clenched and her brain felt as if it was seizing.

Inherently she knew that this wasn't her dream even though she was witnessing it from her perspective. It wasn't her vision. She was seeing from someone else's point of view. She watched as the vision shifted and approached a man from behind. He was working on a car part in the garage and seemed oblivious to the fact that he wasn't alone.

Something made a sound on the cement floor, and the man turned quickly. Ivy recognized him right away. It was Karen's father.

"What are you doing here?" Don asked, annoyed.

No one answered. Ivy opened her mouth in an attempt to communicate with Don, but no sound would come out.

"What in the hell are you doing?" Don's tone shifted from anger to fear and he took a step away from Ivy. That's when Ivy realized she – er, whoever's head she invaded – was holding a knife.

"Don't do this," Don spat. "What ... no ... don't!"

Ivy fought to break from the vision when the blood came, and it took all of her willpower to manage it. She banged her shoulder hard against the counter in her haste to scramble away. When she finally found the strength to move, the tenuous thread tying her to a killer snapped.

"What's wrong?" Max asked, appearing at Ivy's side. "You're as white as a ghost. I saw you go pale and tried talking to you, but it was as if you couldn't see or hear me."

"I ... saw something," Ivy rasped out, gripping Max's hand. "I saw Don Merriman."

"Doing what?"

"Dying."

Max took a moment to absorb the news and then placed his hand on the back of Ivy's head to steady her. "Okay. I believe you. We need to call Jack, though."

"And tell him what?" Ivy was bordering on hysterical. "I can't tell him I magically witnessed a man's murder. He'll lock me up."

"He will not," Max argued. "He'll do everything in his power to protect you. We have to call him. What you saw might not have happened yet. Don could still be alive."

That hadn't occurred to Ivy. "But … ."

"No." Max offered his sister a firm headshake. "It has to be done."

Ivy knew he was right and she reluctantly crawled to the front of the greenhouse to retrieve her purse. She dug inside for her cell phone and stared at it for a moment before hitting Jack's name on her contact list.

He picked up on the first ring. "Do you miss me already?" He was cheerful.

"Jack, I … ." His flirty tone threw off Ivy. How was she supposed to explain this?

As if sensing her uncertainty, Jack instantly sobered. "What is it, honey?"

"I saw something."

"Okay." Jack sounded calm, but Ivy could practically picture him gripping his hands together to keep from flying off the handle. "What did you see?"

"I saw Don Merriman," Ivy replied, opting to get right to the point. Delaying things wouldn't help anyone. "He was being attacked. I … Jack, it was as if I was the one attacking him."

"Well, we both know you're with Max, so it can't be you," Jack said. "Do you know where Don was when this happened?"

"He was in his garage," Ivy said. "There was a car out there … and tools on the wall."

"Okay, honey," Jack said. "We're going to check it out right now. I … you stay with Max."

Ivy wasn't convinced that was the right course of action. "Maybe I should go with you."

"I want you to stay with Max." Jack's voice was soft but firm. "I need to know that you're safe. Do you understand?"

"Yes, but I can't get the sight of Don out of my head," Ivy said. "There was a lot of blood."

"We're going to check that out right now, Ivy," Jack said. "You stay there with Max. I will be in touch as soon as I can."

"Do you promise?"

"I promise," Jack said. "I have to go, though." He moved to disconnect and then stopped himself. "Ivy, everything is going to be okay. I will come to you as soon as I can."

"Okay."

"Everything is going to be okay," Jack repeated. "Trust me."

"I trust you."

Jack wasn't sure she really did, but there was nothing he could do for her now. If Don Merriman was dead – if what she witnessed was true – Jack worried nothing in his life would ever be the same again.

Seventeen

"I don't understand why we're here."

Brian worked overtime to keep his tone even as he followed Jack up Don Merriman's driveway. When the younger officer disconnected from his call with Ivy, he was calm but firm. He didn't elaborate on what the feisty woman said, only stating that it was important they check on Don.

Brian readily agreed to the demand, but he hated being kept in the dark. His discontent only grew as they trudged toward the nondescript house.

"What did she say?"

"She just said we need to check on Don," Jack replied, turning his head as he scanned the house. "We need to look in the garage."

"We don't have a search warrant."

"We're not searching for evidence," Jack said. "We're … ." He had no idea how to explain things so he held his hands palms-up and shrugged. "I can't explain it right now. We need to look in the garage. Only … this house doesn't seem to have a garage."

He was right. The small ranch was an older home and it didn't boast an attached garage. It did, however, have a pole barn that served as a garage located at the back edge of the property. Brian was familiar with the layout because he'd gone fishing with Don a few times over the years.

"There's a barn out back," Brian supplied. "It's kind of like a garage."

"Does it have tools and a car?"

"Yes," Brian answered. "Tell me what's going on."

"Hopefully nothing," Jack said. He was desperate for Ivy's vision to be untrue. He believed in her, though, and he had a sinking feeling they were about to find something terrible. "Lead the way to the barn."

Brian grumbled under his breath as he picked his way to the side of the house and entered the back yard. When they cleared the corner, he pointed at the dilapidated building in question. "There."

Jack was almost relieved when he saw the open door. That emotion dissipated when he couldn't identify movement inside. "Hurry up." He picked up his pace so he was almost jogging, not stopping until he crossed the threshold.

Brian watched him, understandably curious, and then shook his head as he glanced around the empty structure. "There's no one out here."

"We don't know that yet."

Brian heaved out a sigh. "Fine. Don? Are you out here? It's Brian Nixon."

The two men waited for a response. When they didn't get one, Jack pointed toward one side of the vehicle while he headed toward the other. Brian didn't have to be told out loud what his partner wanted.

Jack and Brian slowly walked into the garage, the light dwindling the farther they walked. As he closed in on the back of the barn, Jack saw the one thing he expected – and yet continued to hope against – when a pair of feet poked out from the front of the car.

Jack hurried to the prone figure, trying to push Brian's audible gasp out of his mind as he knelt next to Don. The man had a gaping wound in his chest, blood seeping out on the concrete floor. He pushed his fingers to

Don's neck and found a faint heartbeat. He worried that was the only good news he would get today.

"Call for an ambulance. He's still alive."

"WE NEED to have a talk."

Jack and Brian followed the ambulance to the clinic, remaining mostly silent as the paramedics worked. Jack asked a few questions – mostly about Don's chances – but the paramedics were grim and neither man held out much hope.

Dr. Nesbitt was too busy to talk to them upon their arrival, so they made themselves comfortable in the waiting room. Jack appeared happy with the silence. Brian was another story entirely.

Jack jerked his head in his partner's direction. "Did you say something?"

"Oh, don't do that," Brian chided, wagging a finger. "I think I've been more than a good sport about this. Don Merriman is in the other room fighting for his life. The only reason he has a chance of survival at all is because you knew to look for him."

"Hopefully he'll get lucky."

Brian made a face. "I'm hopeful he'll get lucky, too," he said. "That doesn't mean I don't want to know what's going on. How did you know to look for him?"

Jack's was pale as he ran his hands up and down the front of his blue jeans and shifted in his chair. "I … ." He looked almost tortured.

Brian decided to change his tactics and tone. "I'm on your side, son," he said, lowering his voice. "You know that. I think you believe it. Whatever is going on, though, I need to know what it is. I know you've been hiding something for days. It obviously has to do with Ivy. Talk."

"I don't know if I can tell you," Jack hedged, licking his lips. "It's not exactly my secret and … ."

"And you're worried about exposing Ivy," Brian finished. "I get that you're afraid, but you need to know that I would never hurt Ivy. Why can't you see that?"

"It's not that," Jack said. "I know you wouldn't hurt her. She's so upset, though. I don't know how to help her. I don't want this getting out. She would be crushed if it did."

"Well, Jack, you need to tell me what's going on so I can help," Brian prodded. "We need to protect her together. We're going to have to explain how we knew to look in the garage, son. People are going to ask. We have to get our stories straight."

Jack balked. The last thing he wanted to do was put Brian in a situation where he would have to lie. "Blame it on me."

"Oh, that's cute," Brian intoned. "You're going to tell me the truth. If you don't, then I'm going to confront Ivy. You can't stop me, so don't even try."

"You can't do that," Jack argued. "She would be mortified if she thought you knew."

"I don't think you're giving her enough credit."

"I … dammit!" Jack exploded, slamming his hands down on the chair and hopping to his feet so he could pace. Luckily for them, the lobby was empty so no one witnessed his potential meltdown.

"Tell me," Brian said. "You'll feel better when you do. Then we can start figuring this out."

"You might be sorry I told you when I'm done," Jack warned.

"Try me."

"Okay." Jack let out a shaky breath. "Ever since finding Jeff's body in the maze, Ivy has been having …

visions of sorts, I guess you would say … and she's seen things. That's what happened when she passed out and got sick."

"Uh-huh." Brian remained seated and calm. "Is that what happened today? Did she have a vision of Don?"

"She saw him being stabbed."

"Did she see who was doing it?"

"Um, that's the thing," Jack said, rubbing his chin. "In the two most recent visions, she thinks she's been looking through someone else's eyes."

"Like the killer's?" Brian didn't want to alarm Jack, but he couldn't stop himself from being flabbergasted.

"Yes."

"Well, that's a dilly of a secret," Brian said, shaking his head. "Still, for some reason it doesn't surprise me. Take me through things from the beginning. I need to understand."

That's exactly what Jack did.

"She thought she heard someone saying that he didn't want to die the day at the maze," Jack explained. "We still don't know why she got sick, but for some reason thinking it was supernatural in origin made me feel better. I still can't figure out why."

"Because a real illness is terrifying and this is something that can magically get better," Brian said. "Magically is the key word … and it's one I can't believe I'm saying. I believe you, though, so don't get all … squirrelly."

Jack made a face. "I don't get squirrelly."

"You get squirrelly all of the time when Ivy is involved," Brian said. "She got sick and heard someone talking. Did she see anyone?"

"No," Jack answered. "She said it was dark and then light. She heard the voice and woke up. She got violently ill and felt as if she was on fire."

"You know, it's weird, but I've heard people who have been stabbed in the chest before describe the feeling as if they were caught in a fire and couldn't get out," Brian mused. "Maybe Ivy was somehow … I don't know … empathically linked to Jeff that day."

"I've never considered that, but it's an interesting idea," Jack said. "That doesn't explain the other stuff."

"Tell me about the other stuff."

"We were dream walking the other night and … something weird happened," Jack said. "We went to a castle and were screwing around, but Ivy didn't like it because the bear rug kept staring at her, so we were going to visit a beach. I left first."

"I'm not going to pretend to understand this sharing dreams thing you guys do," Brian said. "I find it weird and invasive. If my wife knew what I dreamed about, she would divorce me."

"It's not like that," Jack said. "We're somehow … cognizant … of what we're doing. When I dream without her, they're regular dreams. When I dream with her, we can control our environment."

"It's still a little freaky," Brian said. "Keep going, though. It's freaky and fascinating at the same time."

"I left her and while she was waiting for me to call her to the new location, Jeff Johnson appeared," Jack said. "She said his skin was gray and his neck was bent at an odd angle. Now, we haven't told anyone what the coroner said about Jeff's neck breaking because someone used a rope to hoist him up onto that cross. I didn't tell Ivy that either. I still haven't."

"Did Jeff speak to her?"

"He just kept repeating that he didn't want to die and Ivy tried to get away from him because she was scared," Jack said. "She bolted awake and was shaking. I tried to calm her down and told her it was just a dream and not to overreact. I didn't believe that, though, and she knew better the next morning."

"It sounds like she's getting echoes from Jeff's final moments," Brian said. His face was serious and he showed no signs of making fun of Jack and his beliefs. "Maybe Jeff realized he was dying and that was his last thought."

"I can believe that," Jack said. "That doesn't explain the two most recent visions."

"Does one have something to do with what happened at the greenhouse yesterday?" Brian asked. "I knew you guys were acting funny for a reason other than your usual flirty banter."

"Yeah, she had another vision the day before yesterday," Jack confirmed. "She went out to the fairy ring and she was sitting there when something kind of … popped into her head. She described it as if she was looking at herself from behind."

"But … how?"

Jack shrugged. "She heard a noise from a tree and believes someone was watching her out there," he said. "She got upset and ran. I happened to be out there looking for her because I brought lunch and she smacked into me while she was running."

"Did you see anyone following her?"

"No, and she was so upset I didn't want to leave her to look," Jack replied. "Max took her out there yesterday, though – and that's one of the reasons we were fighting –

and he says that the leaves behind the tree were disturbed and it looked as if someone ran through them."

"So someone was out there," Brian mused, rolling his neck until it cracked. "Someone was watching her and she managed to get into his head while he was doing it."

"We keep saying 'he,' but it very well could be a she," Jack reminded him.

"I still don't think a woman could've hoisted Jeff's body onto that cross," Brian said. "Even with the added leverage of a rope, there's just no way."

"I happen to agree with you," Jack said. "I don't want to rule out anyone, though. That could end up hurting Ivy if I'm not careful."

"I understand that," Brian said. "What happened today?"

"Ivy was in the greenhouse with Max and she kind of … lost time," Jack said. "She saw herself approaching Don and stabbing him. That's why she called me to check on him."

"So you knew going out there we might be dealing with an injured man. Is that what you're saying?"

"I couldn't send an ambulance out there without visual proof," Jack argued. "How would I have explained that?"

"I'm not casting aspersions on you," Brian said. "I'm just trying to understand what's going on. There's no way we can tell people Ivy had a vision and that's why we headed out to Don's house."

"I don't want you to have to lie for me," Jack said. "That's not fair."

"I'm not lying for you," Brian countered. "I'm lying for Ivy. She's a good girl. She doesn't need this getting out. It's not her fault this is happening."

Jack was relieved, although he remained worried, too. "Why do you think it's happening?"

"I honestly don't know," Brian replied. "There have always been whispers about the women in her family. Felicity is pretty open about being a … witch … and stuff. Maybe there's something in the family genes."

"Has Luna done anything like this?"

"Luna is loony in her own way," Brian said, his smile fond. "If she could do something like that, though, she would've told Ivy. I think Ivy is just special."

"Of course Ivy is special."

"Chill out, Romeo," Brian said. "You know what I mean. If Ivy has somehow tapped into a killer, though, that might mean someone else is seeing through her eyes, too. Have you considered that?"

Jack's mouth went dry. "Um … no."

"I didn't think so," Brian said. "I think that's a possibility. Why else would someone follow Ivy into the woods? Ivy isn't alone, right?"

"Max is with her."

"Keep it that way until we figure out what's going on," Brian said. "Right now, she's going to give us a leg up on this investigation if we use her the correct way."

Jack didn't like Brian's choice of phrasing. "We're not using my girlfriend."

"We might have to utilize her gift," Brian countered. "You know we can't rule that out. For now, we just need to get an update on Don and then see what the state boys find in that garage by way of evidence."

"Speaking of that, here comes Dr. Nesbitt."

Brian joined Jack at the edge of the lobby and waited for the tired looking physician to join them. Nesbitt didn't look happy.

"Is he dead?"

"He's alive, but he's unconscious and has lost a lot of blood," Nesbitt replied. "I considered sending him to the hospital in Traverse City, but they're sending us supplies and a specialist instead. We don't want to risk moving him."

"What's his prognosis?"

"I can't say either way right now," Nesbitt said. "He's unconscious and that's not going to change in the next twenty-four hours. We're fixing up his wounds and getting blood into him.

"He could live or he could die," he continued. "I don't have the answers you're looking for."

"Well, keep us updated," Brian said. "This is obviously tied to Jeff Johnson's death. Moving from one victim to two means this entire community is going to be on edge."

"And just in time for Halloween, too," Nesbitt said. "That will make things even worse."

"There's no doubt about that. Keep us updated."

"You'll be my first call if he wakes up," Nesbitt said. "Trust me. I want this solved as much as you do. This clinic isn't equipped for cases like this. I don't want to lose a patient because we have a madman on the loose."

"That makes two of us."

Eighteen

"You seem tense."

Felicity met Ivy and Max at the front door of the house. She read the stiff set of Max's shoulders right away. When he called and requested she come to Ivy's house to do a ritual cleansing, she was surprised. Max never showed any interest in her work and often pretended he didn't understand her abilities and what she did for a living. He sounded so serious she didn't hesitate to close down her shop for the afternoon and head over, though. One look at Ivy and Max told her she'd made the right decision.

"It's been a long day and it's not even noon yet," Max explained. "I need to run a few errands. Can you stay here with Ivy until Jack gets back?"

"Of course, but I'm still not sure what's going on," Felicity replied.

"Ivy will fill you in." Max pulled Ivy in for a long hug before releasing her. "I'll finish getting the greenhouse in order. You just worry about this."

"Thank you for everything, Max." Ivy mustered a small smile. "You're a great brother ... even when you're a butthead sometimes."

"I know," Max said, ruffling her hair. "I'm going to get a T-shirt made up. The honeys love it when you're a good brother."

Ivy playfully swatted his arm as she watched him head toward his truck in the driveway. She waited until he disappeared onto the road in front of her house before turning her full attention on her aunt. "You didn't need to come. I think Max is being … overly dramatic."

"The fact that you're saying that despite how pale you are tells me that's not the case," Felicity said, ushering Ivy inside. "Why don't you fill me in for starters and we'll go from there, huh?"

Ivy mutely nodded.

"I'll make tea first," Felicity suggested. "Everything is better with tea."

"That's what Jack says about pie."

"Then maybe we'll make a pie, too," Felicity said. "Something tells me you have a lot going on. You can tell me while I do the heavy lifting on the pie. I always think better when my hands are busy."

"That sounds like a plan."

"SO, BASICALLY you're telling me that you think you've managed to crawl into the head of a killer and see through his eyes."

Felicity was surprisingly calm when Ivy finished telling her story. Ivy was on her second glass of tea and Felicity was almost done filling the pie when the younger woman wrapped up the torrid tale.

"I guess so," Ivy said. "It sounds ridiculous when I say it out loud."

"I don't think it's ridiculous."

"Has it ever happened to you?"

"No, but it did happen to my grandmother." Felicity made the announcement in a calm manner, as if she was telling Ivy her great-grandmother made the best jam in five counties instead of the fact that she was psychic. "She hopped into quite a few heads, if you believe the stories, that is."

"I've never heard those stories," Ivy said, knitting her eyebrows together. "All I ever heard about Great-Grandma is that she was mean and liked to boss around people. Mom says I remind her of Great-Grandma. I thought it was a compliment ... until now."

Felicity snickered. "I think it is a compliment," she said. "My grandmother was a wonderful woman. You're a wonderful woman, too. This is simply a new ... twist ... in your story."

"Twist? It's a lot worse than a twist."

"How so?"

The question confused Ivy. "How can you ask that? I'm seeing through a killer's eyes. Jack is going to lock me up in the nuthouse and run as far away as possible."

Felicity's giggle was enough to set Ivy's teeth on edge.

"Jack is going to do nothing of the sort," Felicity said. "He thinks you walk on water. This is just an addition to the magic you've already shown yourself to be in possession of."

Ivy was frustrated. "What magic?"

"What magic?" Felicity made an exaggerated "well, duh" face. "Girl, you've been dream walking with your boyfriend for months. You saw a ghost. You've always been able to sense the emotions of others. Now you're having psychic flashes. It's hardly surprising."

"Maybe it's not surprising to you, but it feels overwhelming to me," Ivy argued. "I just want a normal life."

"Well, you're not normal, so that's an unreasonable wish," Felicity said, adopting a pragmatic tone. "Why would you possibly want to be normal when you're extraordinary?"

"I don't feel extraordinary."

"That's because you're mired in self-doubt and unsure how to proceed," Felicity said. "The truth is, you're intrigued by what's happening. The worry you're feeling has to do with Jack and your family. You think they're going to turn their backs on you when they find out. Nothing could be further from the truth."

"Max couldn't get away from me fast enough after what happened in the greenhouse," Ivy said. "He's afraid of me. He thinks I'm weird."

"He knows you're weird and he doesn't care because he's weird, too," Felicity corrected. "He loves you and he always will. He's your best friend, in a way. Although Jack has kind of taken up that spot in your life, now that I think about it. Do Jack and Max get along?"

The change in topics threw Ivy for a loop. "They get along fine. Max is annoying to everyone and Jack thinks it's funny."

"That's good," Felicity said. "I was worried Max might be jealous of Jack taking up so much of your time."

"Max is just happy that Jack isn't competing with him for women."

"That Max is a pip," Felicity said, chuckling. "I can't wait until he finds a woman to knock him on his ass. Your life got so much better when Jack did the same to you."

"I … really like … Jack," Ivy said, her heart flipping. "He's being so understanding now, but there's no way he'll be able to put up with this over the long haul. He's going to crumble under the pressure. We both know it."

"I don't know that. In fact, I think the opposite is true."

"I'm too weird," Ivy said, her eyes filling with tears. "I'll chase him away."

"Jack will never leave you," Felicity said. "He's too in love with you. You've made his life better and he knows it. You need to stop this. You're not an insecure person.

"Now, I understand that things changing so quickly has you in a tailspin," she continued. "Once things settle down, you'll realize you're being ridiculous and accept Jack's love. Until then, though, I'm here to offer you a little bit of help."

"And how are you going to do that?"

"I'm going to cleanse this house and put up wards," Felicity replied, not missing a beat. "That will allow you to keep getting in other people's heads – especially the killer's – but not let them follow you home."

"Can you really do that?"

"I'm a witch, dear," Felicity replied, winking. "I can do anything."

"Well, I'm up for trying anything," Ivy said. "I'm scared."

"I know you are," Felicity said, clucking sympathetically. "You'll feel stronger in a few days. This is a lot to take in. I'm sure you'll do it with aplomb, though."

"I think you're giving me way too much credit."

"And I think you're being a tad whiny, so we both have our crosses to bear," Felicity said, her eyes twinkling. "Let's put this pie in the oven and get started, shall we? I want to be done in a timely fashion so I can watch *American Horror Story* tonight."

"You watch *American Horror Story*?" Ivy was dumbfounded.

"There's a lot you don't know about me, dear," Felicity said. "Let's make sure there's a lot that no one else can inadvertently find out about you because of your leaky mind gaps, shall we? Protection in this instance is the most important thing. You'll see."

HONEY, I'm home ... and I brought you dinner."

Jack smiled as he walked into the house, stilling briefly when he saw Felicity standing next to the counter. He almost did a double take when he caught sight of the amiable woman, but managed to refrain.

"Hello, Jack," Felicity said, beaming at him. She'd been fond of him since the day they met – when she realized his chemistry with Ivy was off the charts and sensed a change in her only niece's life trajectory – and she had no doubts about his fidelity and fortitude.

"Hi, Felicity," Jack said, lowering the bags of food he carried to the counter. "I didn't know you would be here for dinner. I'm not sure I brought enough food, but I can run back to the diner and get more. What would you like?"

"Oh, I'm not staying for dinner," Felicity said, smiling. "I was here to help Ivy with a chore, but we've finished it."

"What chore?" Jack was understandably curious. "And where is Max?"

"Max left several hours ago," Ivy replied. "Before you get angry, he made Aunt Felicity promise to babysit me until you returned. He went back to the greenhouse to finish things up for me."

"Oh, well, I guess that's okay," Jack said, dropping a kiss on Ivy's cheek. Her skin was cool – why he kept worrying about a return of her fever was beyond him – and she had some color to her face. "Tomorrow is the big day and I can't wait to see the greenhouse."

"Yes, Ivy always goes all out," Felicity said. "How was your day at work?"

"Long."

Ivy lifted her blue eyes to Jack's somber brown orbs. "Is Don dead?"

"No, honey."

"Is he going to die?"

Jack didn't want to upset her, but he also vowed to tell her the truth. He had no intention of lying now. "Dr. Nesbitt doesn't know," he said. "He's going to be unconscious at least for tonight. A specialist from Traverse City arrived about an hour after we got Don to the hospital. I simply don't know.

"What I do know is that he wouldn't have even had a shot at surviving if it wasn't for you," he continued. "You saved him. You should be proud of yourself."

"I'm not sure I did anything to be proud of."

"Nonsense," Felicity interjected. "You didn't let your fear and worry that Jack will dump you because you're different overwhelm you. Instead you did the right thing and called him so he could help Don. That's certainly something to be proud of."

Ivy's mouth dropped open as her eyes narrowed to dangerous slits. "I can't believe you just said that."

"I can't either," Jack said, rubbing his chin. "I think I know why you said it, though."

"I said it because Ivy is too stubborn to admit it herself," Felicity said. "She's letting the worry make her sick, and I knew you would want to know, Jack."

"Thank you for that," Jack said. "Ivy and I are going to have a talk the second you leave."

"I figured you would," Felicity said, chuckling as she moved to Ivy's side and kissed her niece's cheek. Ivy refused to return the gesture and instead stood with her arms crossed over her chest. "You'll forgive me eventually. When you do, I'll have a pot of tea ready for you at the store."

"What else were you doing here?" Jack asked, escorting her to the door. "I mean … other than taking over Max's babysitting duties, that is?"

"I don't need a babysitter!"

Jack ignored Ivy's outburst. "Were you here for a specific reason?"

Felicity studied him for a moment, almost as if she was trying to gauge his worth. "I was here because Ivy is going through something she doesn't understand and ultimately believes is terrible," she replied. "I don't happen to believe that – and she's not the first in our family to discover that she has this gift."

"She'll be okay, right?"

"She'll be fine once she reins in her emotions," Felicity said, offering Jack a kind smile. She adored the fact that his mind went to Ivy's health before anything else. "I put up a few wards and burned some sage to cleanse the house. She shouldn't have to worry about anyone else invading her dreams again."

"What about the other?"

"Her going into a killer's head? She should still be able to do that. Hopefully, with time, she'll even learn how to control it."

"Thank you," Jack said. "I really appreciate all you've done for her."

"I really appreciate all you've done for her," Felicity said. "That's why I baked you a pie."

Jack's eyes lit up. "Seriously?"

"Yes. It's cooling on the counter."

Jack shifted his eyes and found what he was looking for, a small smile playing at the corner of his lips. "You really know how to make my night, don't you?"

"I think I do," Felicity said. "Now you just need to make her night. Can you do that?"

"I'm on it."

JACK made a big show of opening the food containers and placing them in the center of the table as Ivy stood a few feet away and watched. She was still mortified by her aunt's big mouth, and she couldn't help but feel she should do something – like apologize or run and hide in her bedroom – but Jack seemed at ease when he motioned for her to sit.

"I got you the veggie wrap, French fries, onion rings, those apple rings you like, and a side of mashed potatoes because I didn't know what you would be in the mood for," Jack volunteered.

Ivy couldn't help but smile. "Are you trying to fatten me up?"

"I'm trying to make sure you have everything you need," Jack countered. "Before we eat, though, we need to talk."

Ivy's heart rolled. "We do?"

"Wipe that look off your face right now," Jack ordered. "That look is what we need to talk about. I don't want to see it again – not because you're worried about me breaking up with you because you're different, at least. Do you understand?"

Ivy wet her lips. "Jack ... ."

"No." Jack's headshake was firm. "I am not going to break up with you over this. I don't care that it's new and you're still feeling your way around. I like that you're different. That's the reason I fell ... I mean, that's the reason I was attracted to you in the first place."

Jack's tongue trip wasn't lost on Ivy, and she realized what he almost said before stopping himself. Max was right, she internally mused. Jack wanted to say it but was afraid. They were exactly alike ... which was a frightening thought.

"I don't mean to be insecure," Ivy said, choosing her words carefully. "It's just ... now that I have you, I'm terrified I'm going to lose you. You're only going to be able to put up with so much before it's too much."

"That's not true," Jack said. "It will never be too much. That's beside the point, though. I don't blame you for this. I'm not angry. I'm not put out. I'm simply trying to understand, just like you.

"We're going to muddle through this together, Ivy Morgan," he continued. "You can't get rid of me. Don't even try. Do you understand?"

Ivy pressed her lips together and nodded.

"Good. Now eat your dinner because I'm going to go nuts with that pie in exactly thirty minutes."

Ivy couldn't stop herself from giggling. "Thank you."

The words were so simple – so heartfelt – Jack's heart hitched. "Honey, thank you for being you," he said. "Don't worry about things like that, though. That drives me crazy."

"Okay."

"Now eat your dinner," Jack said. "That pie is calling to me. I might take that pie with us when we dream tonight, in fact. Prepare yourself. We're going to a pie-eating contest tonight, honey."

Nineteen

"How did you tell your wife you loved her the first time?"

Jack's bungled attempt at reassuring Ivy the previous night still bothered him the next day as he made the trek across the town square to the clinic on foot with Brian. The words were out of his mouth before he could give serious thought to whether or not it was wise to bring up the subject.

For his part, the older cop was taken aback by the question. He didn't see it coming. "Excuse me?"

Jack wasn't bothered by Brian's incredulous tone. "How did you tell your wife you loved her the first time?"

"I think you need to be more specific," Brian said. "I just kind of blurted out the words and then hung my head until she said it back. Well, first she laughed at me for being a goofball and then she said it back. Is that what you're looking for?"

"You didn't plan something special?" Jack asked, genuinely curious. "I mean … you didn't take her out to dinner or for a moonlit stroll or anything? That seems … somehow anticlimactic."

"Oh, boy," Brian muttered, tugging up the collar of his coat to ward off the chill as the two men closed the distance to the clinic. "You're just a bundle of nerves, aren't you?"

"I almost told Ivy I loved her last night, but it didn't happen," Jack said. "It almost escaped, though, like my tongue was a mouse in a trap and it couldn't break free fast enough."

Brian barked out a laugh, delighted. "You're a real trip sometimes. I just … you're so much work."

"That's what I tell Ivy several times a week. About her, though, not me. I think I'm great."

"I think that's what every man thinks until he finds the right woman to knock him down a peg or two," Brian said. "As for planning something special, no, I didn't do that. I thought I was going to do that, but the words kind of spilled out before I got the chance."

"Do you think your wife would've liked a special evening to mark the occasion?"

"I think my wife was just happy I finally admitted it because things were getting tense between us at the time," Brian replied. "This was thirty years ago, mind you, and she told me she was starting to think I was never going to admit it – which meant I was never going to propose – and she was considering breaking up with me before it happened because she didn't think the relationship was going anywhere."

The words had a sobering effect on Jack. "Do you think she really would've broken up with you?"

"No."

"Do you think she would've picked a fight to force your hand?"

"No."

"So what is the moral of this story?" Jack asked, frustrated. "Did you at least feel better after you did it?"

"I felt a lot better after I did it," Brian confirmed. "I also felt like an idiot for not doing it sooner."

"I feel more lost now than I did when we started this conversation," Jack groused. "Do you think I should tell Ivy I love her?"

"I'm stunned you haven't done it already," Brian answered honestly. "You two can't stop cooing at one another when you're feeling lovey-dovey. You both suffer from diarrhea of the mouth when you're fighting, too. It should've easily spilled out then."

"I feel like the longer I wait, the harder it is to tell her," Jack said. "I should've told her when I first realized it, but I thought it was too soon then. I still think it might be too soon. We've only been dating for a few months. What do you think? Is it too soon?" Jack was a babbling mess today. There was no way around that.

"I knew I loved my wife two weeks after we started dating and I waited six months to tell her," Brian said. "She wasn't happy about that. She was even more unhappy when I finally said it right after … well, you know."

Jack was horrified when he realized what Brian was referring to. "Seriously?"

"Yeah. I can't offer you a lot of advice on the subject, but never do it right after you do … that. The women don't like it and think you're only saying it because you briefly lost your mind. I had to say it another twenty times before the wife believed me."

"I wasn't considering telling her like that," Jack said. "I thought maybe I would take her out for a nice dinner and then tell her."

"Like … here's a steak and I love you?"

Jack snickered. "Kind of. Ivy won't eat steak, though."

"I keep forgetting she's a vegetarian," Brian said. "Does that make your life difficult when making dinner plans?"

"She's pretty easy to appease on that front," Jack replied. "She's more than willing to settle for a salad. We were in Traverse City a few weeks ago and I wanted Red Lobster. You never realize how few choices there are for someone who won't eat meat in a place like that."

"What did she get?"

"They went off the menu and made her a vegetarian pasta so it wasn't terrible, but I felt guilty," Jack said. "That did not stop me from eating a huge steak, lobster tail, and crab legs, though."

"Hey, a man has got to eat."

Jack smiled, the morning sun bright even as the cold washed over him. Ivy was still asleep when he got out of bed. He snuggled up behind her for a few minutes, relishing the fact that he could hold her as long as he wanted, and then let her rest. He tucked her feet under the covers despite the fact that she always shoved them out again the moment he wasn't looking and pressed a kiss to her cheek before leaving the room. Max was flipping through the newspaper in the kitchen when he left the house.

"I need to tell her," Jack said. "My stomach is twisted in knots because I haven't done it yet."

"Then tell her."

"What if she doesn't say it back?"

"Good grief," Brian muttered. "You're such an idiot. Of course she's going to say it back. Do you want to know what I think your problem is?"

"Not really."

"I think you're problem is that you keep holding back because once you say those words, it makes everything real."

"Everything is already real."

"Mostly, but not entirely," Brian corrected. "Once you say those words, Ivy is truly going to be yours. Perhaps you don't want that."

Jack was affronted. "Of course I want that," he sputtered. "That's all I want. I … how can you even say that?"

"I'm just making an observation." Brian averted his gaze because he didn't want Jack to see the mirth in his eyes. If the younger police officer realized Brian was merely messing with him in an effort to propel him forward, he would fight the effort out of pure stubbornness.

"She's already mine," Jack said. "She's my … whole heart. I'm going to tell her."

"You should."

"I'm going to do it."

"Good."

Jack sucked in a calming breath as they hit the front door of the clinic. "I don't even know why I confide in you sometimes."

"Life is a mystery, son," Brian said. "Speaking of mysteries, though, we should see if we can make some progress on this one. We still have a murderer running free, and that's not good for anyone."

"HOW IS he?" Jack asked Dr. Nesbitt as they walked through the door. The doctor must've been expecting them because he was standing in the lobby when they entered.

"He's awake, actually," Nesbitt replied. "He's not out of the woods, though."

"What does that mean?"

"It means that whoever stabbed him either didn't know what he was doing or didn't want Don to die," Nesbitt replied. "I was talking with the specialist this morning – he's staying out at the Graves Bed and Breakfast on the highway until Don can either be transferred or upgraded – and he thinks that someone purposely poked Don in an odd place."

"That sounds vaguely dirty," Jack said, earning a sharp glare from Brian. "Continue, though."

"Instead of stabbing Don here – where the blade would go through the heart – whoever attacked him stabbed him through his ribcage," Nesbitt said, demonstrating the manner of the attack on Brian. "I don't know anyone who would attack that way."

"It is a weird way to try to kill someone," Brian said, rubbing the back of his neck. "I mean, if we were talking about a short individual, maybe. Don isn't tall, though, and that means if someone was aiming high to stab him and accidentally got him in the rib area, they would have to be like four feet tall."

"Or on their knees," Jack supplied.

"Huh." Brian was intrigued at the thought. "Why would someone be on their knees for an attack?"

"That's a good question," Jack said. "The only thing I can think of is that perhaps someone crawled behind the car so Don wouldn't see him before the attack and have time to run. Maybe Don caught sight of him before he had a chance to get to his feet."

"That's as plausible a theory as anything else," Brian said. "I'm curious about the wound, though. If it's not in a terribly bad location, why is Don in such rough shape?"

"Well, he lost a lot of blood," Nesbitt said. "If you guys were even five minutes later than you were I don't think he would've made it. Besides that, though, he's also got significant liver damage that isn't associated with the wound."

Jack read between the lines and surmised what Nesbitt was inferring. "He's an alcoholic."

Nesbitt nodded. "His wife denies it. She was here earlier and had to return home to lay down because she had a headache, but he's clearly been doing some heavy drinking."

"I think Melanie – that's his wife – does quite a bit of drinking, too," Brian said. "That's my memory of spending time with them, at least. Is he going into liver failure?"

"Not so far, but we're watching him closely," Nesbitt replied. "The good news is that the human liver is one of those organs that can bounce back if it's not too late. The bad news is that Don's wound has compounded the issue."

"So, what's your treatment?" Jack asked.

"We're treating him normally right now," Nesbitt answered. "He doesn't have access to alcohol here. Once he's feeling stronger, we'll have a long talk about the drinking. He'll be detoxing here because he doesn't have another choice, though."

"That's probably for the best," Brian said. "Can we see him?"

"Yes, he's expecting you," Nesbitt said. "You need to keep the visit short, though. He needs his rest. Try to keep it to as few questions as possible."

"We really only need to ask one big question."

Jack and Brian followed Nesbitt into Don's room. The shades were drawn to limit the light and the television was off. The only noise came from the rhythmic sound of the machines next to the bed.

Don's eyes were closed when the police officers entered the room. Nesbitt was gentle as he shuffled to the man's side and carefully touched his arm.

"Don, Brian Nixon and Jack Harker are here to talk to you," Nesbitt said. "Do you feel up to talking to them?"

Don was slow to open his eyes, and when he did, it took him a moment to focus on his guests. He grunted out his assent as he struggled to find a comfortable position, ultimately giving up and remaining on his back as Jack and Brian moved toward him.

"We don't want to take up too much of your time, Don, but we need to know what happened," Brian prodded.

"I don't remember," Don rasped. "I was in the garage. I was working on the carburetor and … that's it. Everything goes blank."

"Do you think someone was in the garage with you?"

"I don't know."

"What were you doing before you went to the garage to work on the carburetor?" Jack asked. "Were you on the phone with anyone? Did you talk to anyone?"

"Just Melanie," Don replied. "She called from the supermarket to see if I wanted steak or chicken for dinner. I told her I wanted steak – but only if it was on sale – and then she hung up.

"I sat in the chair watching the news for a few minutes because I wanted to hear what they were saying about Jeff's death and then … I went out to the garage," he continued. "I don't really remember walking out there, though. I know I arrived because I remember working."

"That's okay," Brian said. "You might remember more when you've had a little more rest."

"I'm sure it was Dave Johnson," Don said. "You need to arrest him."

Brian kept his smile in place as he locked gazes with Don. "You just said you don't remember who attacked you."

"That doesn't mean I don't know who did it," Don argued. "It was Dave. You saw him at the funeral home. He wants me dead."

"But … why?" Brian asked. "What would he get out of your death?"

"He wants Karen's baby," Don said. "He told everyone at the funeral home he was going to take it. The only thing standing in his way is me because he knows I'll help Karen with money and babysitting."

Brian and Jack exchanged a quick look. As far as motives went, it was kind of weak. That didn't mean it was out of the realm of possibility.

"We're going to talk to Dave right now, and if he's guilty, we'll arrest him," Brian said. "I don't want you to worry about that. Just … relax. If you remember anything, tell Dr. Nesbitt. He'll give us a call."

"I don't need to remember," Don said, his stubbornness apparent even as his strength flagged and his eyes lost the battle to remain open. "I know it was Dave. He threatened that he was going to come after my family. I guess he did it."

"We're going to talk to him," Brian soothed. "You have my word he won't touch Karen's baby. Just rest.

You're going to need your strength for when you become a grandfather."

Twenty

"How do I look?"

Despite her troubles over the past few days, Ivy found she was still excited to celebrate Halloween. There was nothing that could diminish her delight with the season, and even though the actual holiday was still two days away, that didn't mean she wouldn't enjoy tonight's festivities. This was her favorite time of the year, after all. She wouldn't let anything ruin her first Halloween with Jack.

Max, who was studying his own costume in Ivy's bathroom mirror, shifted his eyes from the vampire countenance he'd painted on his face and grinned when he saw his sister's costume. She'd opted for a long black dress with a slit up the leg, orange and black leggings – which looked to be thigh-highs, if the slit was to be believed – peeking out from the split fabric, and over-the-top makeup. The outfit was complete thanks to a conical hat.

"You look cute," Max said. "You look a little slutty, too."

Ivy balked. "Hey!"

"I don't remember that costume being quite that … risqué … last year," Max pointed out. "There definitely wasn't a slit."

"That's because this is a new dress," Ivy shot back. "The old one … was falling apart."

"Yeah, I can see that," Max deadpanned. "You wore it once a year for five years so … yup. Five times totally ruined it."

"Shut up," Ivy grumbled, smacking her brother's arm. "Do you always have to be such a pain?"

"I believe that being a pain is listed as my top job in the Big Brother Handbook," Max replied, not missing a beat. "Tell me about the costume, though. Now that I look at it closer, it seems to be cut a little lower than the other one, too. I'm guessing this is all for Jack's benefit."

Ivy glanced down at her dress, frowning. There was no visible cleavage. She would never risk that for a children's event. "What are you talking about?"

"Ha, ha. Made you look."

Ivy lashed out to smack Max and missed, growling when he hopped out of range and hurried down the hallway toward the living room. She gave chase, only stopping when the front door opened, making room for Jack to enter.

"I'm going to kill you," Ivy warned, laughing when Jack caught her before she could launch herself at her brother. "You're dead the second Jack isn't around to protect you."

"Oh, I'm so scared," Max said, feigning as if his hands were shaking. "Whatever will I do?"

"Leave your sister alone or I'll thump you," Jack warned, making sure Ivy was firmly on her feet before he released her and took a long gander at her costume. The smile that split his face was wide and delighted. "You look … smoking hot."

Ivy blushed at the appraising way he looked her over. "Thank you."

"Oh, and I was just telling her she looked slutty," Max said.

"Knock that off," Jack said, extending a finger. "She looks adorable."

"Did you see the slit?"

"That was the first thing I saw," Jack said, tickling Ivy's ribs before he bent over to kiss her cheek. "I didn't realize you guys would already be in your costumes. I'm obviously running late."

"If I were you, I would just go as a tired police officer," Max said. "You're already in costume for that."

"You do look exhausted," Ivy said, running her finger over his cheek. "You only texted once this afternoon and I was still asleep when you left so I missed our usual breakfast together. How did things go?"

"Yeah, I'm sorry about that, but we were pretty busy," Jack said, sighing as he sat in the armchair before tumbling her into his lap. He buried his face in her hair as he hugged her, taking solace in her warmth and strength before lifting his head. "Don Merriman is awake."

"He is?" Ivy was relieved. "Did he tell you who attacked him?"

"He doesn't remember," Jack answered. "He said he remembers being in the house and talking to his wife while she was shopping. Then he remembers being in the garage. Everything else is a blank."

"Is there a possibility he'll remember more as he recovers?" Max asked, cutting himself a slice of pie in the kitchen. "That happens to people, right?"

"Don't eat my pie," Jack snapped. "That's mine."

"Too late," Max said, forking a huge mound into his mouth and chewing as Jack glared at him.

"I'll make you another one," Ivy said. "I'll even make you a pumpkin one, too, just because you're so cute."

"Oh, and I thought my day was going to be terrible," Jack said, grinning as Max mimed throwing up in the adjacent room. "Where was I in the story, though?"

"You were about to tell us if Don could remember who attacked him later," Max prodded.

"Right. He could remember, but the problem we have is that Don is convinced that Dave Johnson is the one who attacked him," Jack said. "He won't give it up and I'm worried if he does remember it's Dave, we won't be able to trust the information because he's already convinced himself that's the truth without actual memories to back it up. It could end up being a self-fulfilling prophecy."

"Why would Dave want to kill Don?" Max asked. "Does he even have a motive?"

"The baby," Ivy supplied. "Dave was threatening to take it away from Karen at the funeral home. Don was angry and they said some nasty things to one another. Maybe Dave did it because Don would be a hurdle in his efforts to claim the baby."

"That's what Don said, and we're not ruling it out," Jack said. "We went to Dave's house to talk to him and he claims that he was working in the insurance office at the time Don was attacked."

"Does that check out?"

"The office was closed yesterday," Jack replied. "That's either incredibly convenient or inconvenient, depending on which side of this you're on."

"Which side are you on?" Max asked.

"I'm not picking a side because I don't want to make any mistakes," Jack said. "Whoever did this is after Ivy. He was in the woods following her and he broke into the greenhouse."

"What about the greenhouse?" Ivy asked. "Did you get a match on the fingerprints?"

"We haven't gotten results back yet," Jack said, rubbing his nose against Ivy's soft cheek. "Right now we're in a holding pattern."

"You can hold me in your pattern," Ivy teased.

"Oh, honey, I'm going to hold you in a multitude of different patterns tonight."

"And I'm back to wanting to barf," Max said.

"As much as I would like to continue watching you mess with Max, you need to change into your costume," Ivy said. "We have to be over at the greenhouse in twenty minutes to make sure everything is ready for the kids to arrive."

Jack blew out a sigh. "Do I really have to wear a costume?"

"You said you would."

"I know, but … ."

"You don't have to." Ivy cut him off quickly and moved to climb off of his lap. "It's fine. You've had a long day."

She said the words, but Jack could practically feel the disappointment wafting off of her.

"I can't wait to wear the costume," Jack said, holding her hips steady and leaning forward to nuzzle her neck. "Give me ten minutes to change."

"Are you sure?"

"I'm sure this is going to be a great night," Jack replied. "That's the most important thing to me. I'll be right back."

"OKAY, honey, we have a problem."

When Jack stepped into the living room, Max could do nothing but burst out laughing. Since he was drinking a mug of hot chocolate, he spewed the liquid all over the counter and earned a positively hateful glance from Ivy.

"What's the problem?" Ivy asked, her hands landing on her hips as she regarded Jack. "I think you look great."

"Yes, and I think you're messing with me," Jack said, shifting his eyes to Max. "What do you think?"

"I think you're downright handsome," Max said, fighting the urge to guffaw. "In fact, I think you look like you have nine lives … and all of them are fuzzy and have a tail."

Jack pursed his lips as he glanced down at his costume. He appreciated the fact that Ivy got him simple black pants and a shirt for the bulk of his costume. When she brought up the subject of a costume, he agreed as long as she didn't go overboard. It was the felt tail and ears that were giving him pause.

"I don't hate it," Jack said. "I just think maybe we should pick something else."

"We don't have anything else," Ivy said, jutting out her lower lip. "I picked that because I have a black cat and I thought you would look adorable … which you do."

"Honey, it's one thing for you to find me adorable when we're alone," Jack pointed out. "It's quite another for the entire town to find me adorable. I would think that's something you would want to keep all for yourself."

"Oh, that was a brilliant save, man," Max said, snickering. "I mean … it was masterful. Really."

"Shut up, Max," Jack barked.

"So you're saying you don't want to be a cat?" Ivy was obviously annoyed when she crossed her arms over her chest.

"I don't want to be a cat," Jack said.

"He just doesn't want to wear a costume at all," Max said, purposely stoking the flames of Ivy's fury. "He wants to ruin one of your favorite holidays."

"That's not true," Jack protested. "That's just crap. I want to make this night special for her. I really do. I just … I can't go out in public dressed up like a cat. It's not dignified."

"Then take off the costume," Ivy said. "It doesn't matter. I thought you would like it, but obviously I was wrong."

"Ivy." Jack felt helpless. He didn't want to upset her, but he refused to wear the cat costume no matter how pouty she got.

"There's an old costume hanging on my side of the closet," Ivy said. Technically, the entire closet belonged to her, but she made room for some of Jack's items when he started spending almost every night with her. "Maybe that will fit. If not, it doesn't matter. I guess Halloween is ruined."

Jack ran his tongue over his teeth. She didn't seem excited about the other costume, but he was desperate to do something – anything really – to salvage the night. "Just give me a second to look at the other costume," he said. "I'm sure everything will be okay."

"I'm sure you're delusional," Max called to his back. "You might want to see if that new costume has a cup attached."

Jack's back was already to Max so he didn't see the conspiratorial smile the siblings shared as he disappeared into the bedroom. He immediately headed for the closet and scanned the racks where Ivy kept her clothes. He finally found a garment bag at the far end, and when he tugged it out, he found a slip of paper on the zipper. It had a small purple heart on it.

Jack had no idea what it meant, but when he opened the second costume his heart felt like it was expanding in his chest. He tugged out the suede pants and matching vest, grinning when he saw the cowboy hat and fake badge that accompanied the outfit.

Ivy surprised him when she slid into the room. "The boots are on the floor next to mine."

"I can't believe you remembered this," Jack said, his eyes burning. "I … just can't believe it."

"You said you always wanted to be a cowboy cop when you were a kid, but your mother never got you the costume," Ivy said. "It's never too late to live out your childhood dreams, Jack."

"And the cat costume?"

"Well, that was part of my dream," Ivy conceded. "I wanted to see if you would put it on. Max actually wore it a few years ago … and ironically, he scored a lot of tail because women thought he was adorable."

Jack grinned as he studied the costume, and then he took Ivy by surprise when he dropped it and grabbed the front of her dress. He hauled her to him, wrapping his arms around her waist and kissing her cheek as he struggled to maintain his emotions.

"Wow. If this is the reaction I get for finding the perfect costume, I can't wait to see what you do when I make you wear one of those hats that has mistletoe attached to it at Christmas."

"No one has ever listened to me like you do," Jack murmured, brushing a kiss against her ear and sending shivers down her spine. "You really get me … and you understand me … and even though you made me put on the cat costume first, you have no idea how much I appreciate this."

Ivy was touched by the naked emotion on his face. "It's okay," she said, patting his back. "I always wanted to have sex with a cowboy, too."

"Well, honey, then it's going to be a big night for you," Jack teased, dropping a scorching kiss on her mouth before releasing her. "I need to get changed if we're going to make it to the greenhouse on time."

"I'll be with Max in the kitchen," Ivy said, her eyes glazed as she fought off tears. "I'll make sure he doesn't eat the rest of your pie."

Jack watched her go, his heart full. "You already belong to me," he whispered. "I belong to you, too." He knew the time for waiting was over. It was Ivy's favorite time of the year, and he was going to make it even more special by admitting his feelings. For the first time, the thought didn't fill him with fear. It filled him with glee.

It was definitely going to be a big night.

Twenty-One

Ivy practically skipped through the woods as she hurried toward the nursery, forcing Max and Jack to struggle to keep up. Jack was happy as long as he could keep an eye on her, and he chose to fall in step with Max rather than crowd Ivy and potentially bring down her happy mood.

"You seem lost in thought," Max said after a few minutes. "Are you considering challenging me to a gunfight at sundown?"

Jack snorted. "It's Michigan in the fall. The sun has already gone down."

"You're such a killjoy."

"And you're a vampire," Jack said, looking Max up and down. "Is that so you can get close to women and suck on their necks or something?"

Max smiled. "Pretty much."

"You're kind of sick."

"I'm a work in progress," Max clarified. "So are you … although you seem to be making a lot of progress. Just for the record, Ivy was so happy when you liked the costume I thought she was going to cry … but for a good reason."

"Well, I'm not thrilled she made me get into the cat costume first, but I actually always wanted to be a cowboy," Jack said. "My mother didn't like the idea because she didn't want to encourage me to carry a gun. She thought I might like it too much."

Max barked out a laugh. "I guess that backfired on her, huh?"

"Just a little."

Max was in a jovial mood, but he sobered and lowered his voice. "Thank you for being so good to my sister. I don't want to make a thing out of it or anything, but you've been great to her and I really appreciate it."

Jack was surprised by Max's earnest statement. "I love her." The moment he uttered the words he felt as if a weight had been lifted off his shoulders. Sure, he hadn't related his feelings to Ivy yet, but somehow admitting it to Max was just as difficult.

"I know you do," Max said, not missing a beat. "I told her that."

"You did?"

"She loves you, too," Max said. "She wants to tell you but is worried you won't feel it … or maybe that you'll think she's pressuring you. I told her that was ridiculous, but you know women."

"I don't know anything about women," Jack said. "I do feel like I know Ivy, though, and I've been worrying about the same thing myself. Tonight, though, when I saw that costume … I just knew that it was going to be okay."

Even though the path between the house and nursery was dark, Jack didn't miss the wide smile flitting across Max's chiseled face.

"You and Ivy are hilarious and fairly dramatic when you want to be, but I'm pretty sure you're going to be happy together," Max said. "You get her and you don't try to change her. I always worried she would fall for someone who wanted to mold her into someone else. I don't worry about that with you."

"I don't want anyone else," Jack said. "I like her just the way she is. Sure, she's a little mouthy, but I even enjoy it when she flies off the handle."

"And you think I'm sick."

"You *are* sick."

"Then you're just as sick as me, buddy," Max said, snickering. "Still, I'm so happy for you and Ivy I almost feel jealous."

Jack lifted an eyebrow, surprised. "Jealous of what?"

"Don't ever tell Ivy I said this because I'll deny it and then beat you senseless, but sometimes when I watch the two of you together, I get this weird feeling I can't describe," Max said. "I think it might be yearning."

"I thought you were happy with your lot in life?" Jack challenged. "You've got honeys on every corner, right?"

"Yeah, and I enjoy not being tied down," Max said. "I'm pretty sure I'm not ready to commit to someone full time, and that's okay. I've got plenty of time to settle down when I'm finally ready.

"The thing is, I didn't think I would ever want to settle down until I saw you and Ivy together," he continued. "The other day, for example, you were sitting in the living room reading a magazine and she poured herself a cup of tea. Even though there was plenty of room on the couch, she sat on your lap.

"You didn't invite her to do it, but you seemed to expect her to do it," he said. "You lifted the magazine and made room for her, kissed her cheek, and then proceeded to flip through the magazine together. You never said one word to each other, and yet you were completely joined and happy."

"I don't remember that, but I'll take your word for it," Jack said. "I feel … in tune with her … for lack of a better way to describe it. I didn't know it was possible. There are times I reach out to grab her hand and realize she's already reaching for my hand.

"I like it when she puts her head on my shoulder, or whispers something silly that only I'll get," he continued. "I feel sad when I can't touch her … and before your head goes in a dirty direction, I mean that in a respectful way. I love her. I think I've loved her from the moment I met her."

"You guys have something special, that's for sure," Max said, bobbing his head. "The dream walking thing is weird. When I first heard about it, I thought Ivy was making it up. I couldn't understand how anyone could think they were sharing interactive dreams."

"And now?"

"I think it's obviously happening," Max replied. "I don't know how to explain it, but something is different about Ivy over the past few months. She seems … ."

"Magical," Jack supplied.

Max snorted. "I was going to say powerful, but I guess that fits," he said. "She's definitely growing into something, and I'm thankful you're there to grow with her instead of trying to stifle her."

"I'll never leave her," Jack offered. "I won't do what I did that day at the hospital after she was shot again. That was wrong. I want you to know that. I made a mistake and I will never do it again."

"I know that," Max said, his eyes kind when they locked with Jack's contemplative brown orbs. "I was really angry with you that day and said some horrible things. I don't regret saying them, but I know you were hurting, too. It's okay.

"Ivy understands and she forgives you," he continued. "I forgive you, too. I don't doubt for a second that you love my sister. I know you'll always take care of her."

"I will," Jack confirmed. "It's not just for her, though. It's for me, too. She somehow ... makes me feel whole."

"Well, that's great," Max said. "I think you do the same for her."

"I hope so."

"I know so," Max said, running his tongue over his teeth as the nursery popped into view and he squared his shoulders. "Never tell my sister we had this chick conversation. I'll never live it down."

Jack chuckled. "Your secret is safe with me."

"Your secret is safe with me, too," Max said.

"What secret?"

"The love secret."

"That's not a secret," Jack said. "I'm telling her tonight. I'm going to wait until after the party and then ... tell her. I have no idea how, but I'm not holding back any longer. I don't care if people think it's too soon. I want her to know how I feel."

"I'm glad for you both."

"Thanks."

The two men exchanged awkward smiles and then Max cleared his throat to signify that the time for being schmaltzy was over. "So ... um ... do you want to help me pick out a honey?"

Jack rolled his eyes. "I'm sure you're fully capable of doing that yourself."

"That's not what I asked."

Jack blew out a sigh. "Fine. I just want to keep an eye on Ivy all night. As long as we stick close to her, I'll help you pick out a woman."

Max's smile was impish. "Let the games begin."

THE SOUND of terrified screams as Michael led another group of children through the haunted greenhouse an hour later was music to Ivy's ears. She bounded toward Jack, who had his head bent together with Max as they leaned against a tree, and grabbed his hand.

"What are you doing?"

Jack couldn't help but smile at her sparkling eyes, excitement wafting in his direction as her intoxicating presence almost barreled him over. "I'm talking to your brother. What are you doing?"

"Did you hear the kids screaming? They're having a good time."

"I heard them," Jack said. "Why aren't you in there showing them around? You've done like five groups in a row."

"I have, but I needed a small break," Ivy admitted. "I'm starting to lose my voice."

"That's because you do that scary raspy thing when you give the tours," Max said, winking at a blonde as she walked past him. She was dressed in a genie costume and even though it was cold, she didn't bother to cover up her midriff. "You should talk like a normal human being."

Ivy made a face, which was completely lost on her brother because he couldn't be bothered to look in her direction. "I saw that."

"You saw what?"

"The way you looked at Ally Peterson," Ivy replied. "She's dating Jordan Turner, so don't get any ideas."

Max finally shifted his gaze from the blonde in question and focused on his sister. "She's *dating* Jordan. She's not married. Heck, she's not even engaged. That means she's open for offers."

"No, it doesn't."

"Yes, it does."

"Jack and I are only dating and we're not open for offers," Ivy pointed out. "I think Jordan and Ally are the same way."

"Oh, I don't know," Max replied. "You might not be open for offers. That doesn't mean Jack isn't."

"Don't drag me into this," Jack warned. "I refuse to play that game." He turned his warm eyes to his girlfriend. "I'm definitely not open for offers from anyone but you."

"That's very good to know," Ivy said, giggling when Jack tugged her closer so he could give her a hug. "You're definitely going to have a cauldron full of offers later tonight."

"Oh, and you just made my night, honey," Jack said, kissing her cheek. "A cauldron, though?"

"That's what we're using to bob for apples in the back of the greenhouse," Ivy replied. "Later on I thought we could put a blanket on the floor and bob for something else."

"Oh, I'm totally going to barf," Max lamented. "What is wrong with you two? I'm standing right here."

Jack ignored Max's theatrics. "I think you just gave me something new to look forward to," he said, rubbing his thumb against Ivy's cheek. "You're going to keep your witch dress on, right?"

"Oh, geez," Max muttered. "Now I'm going to have visions of you two playing cowboys and witches going through my head all night."

"Oh, please," Ivy intoned. "You're going to spend exactly twenty minutes searching for a honey and then disappear with the first one that crosses your path. You're not going to have anything but your own antics going through your head."

Max beamed. "That does sound nice, doesn't it? I can take my honey for a walk to that little field across the way. The moon is beautiful tonight. It almost looks as if there's some red on it."

Ivy shifted here eyes to the sky. She hadn't noticed the moon tonight. "It's a full moon. It's a blood moon."

"What's a blood moon?" Jack asked, genuinely curious.

"It's a witch thing Aunt Felicity used to tell us about when we were kids," Max answered. "It has something to do with four eclipses happening in a row."

"It's supposed to be magical," Ivy said, using her fingertip to trace Jack's palm. "It's supposed to be a powerful time when almost anything can happen. I forgot about it. I used to pay attention when I was a kid, but … ."

"But what?" Jack prodded.

"But nothing," Ivy said, shaking herself out of her momentary reverie. "It's stupid."

"Tell me," Jack prodded.

"It's just … for a second I thought the blood moon might be a reasonable answer for why I've been seeing things," Ivy explained. "Magic is supposed to be really strong during a blood moon transition. Supposedly, if you believe the old tales, good magic and bad magic can bleed over into one another during a blood moon."

Jack slipped a strand of Ivy's hair behind her ear as he considered the statement. "Do you believe the old tales?"

"I'm not sure I even remember the old tales," Ivy admitted. "I didn't remember the eclipses until Max mentioned the moon looked red. I'm not sure how much of that stuff I believe."

"Really?" Jack challenged. "Even after everything you've seen?"

"I don't know what to think," Ivy admitted. "All I know is that I don't want this night to be ruined. If I think too much about the other stuff, the night will go down the toilet."

"Well, no one wants that," Jack said, giving her another hug and kiss on the cheek before releasing her. "I promised to help your brother find a honey, but I swear I'm going to take a bunch of kids through the greenhouse with you before the night is over."

"Okay," Ivy said, shaking off the remnants of her doldrums and returning to her happy countenance. "How about I take the next tour through alone and then you can join me after that?"

"That sounds like a plan."

"That sounds like a really boring way to spend an evening," Max corrected.

Ivy cuffed him before skirting away, giggling when Max scorched her with a death glare. She practically skipped over to the greenhouse, disappearing around the edge of the building so she could enter the structure through the side door and not draw unnecessary attention to herself.

Jack watched her leave, his eyes lingering even after she disappeared from sight. When he finally turned his gaze back to Max, he found the other man staring at him. "What?"

"You'd better tell my sister soon, because you're so goofy and in love it's starting to give me a sour stomach."

"I'll get right on that."

Twenty-Two

Ivy was lost in thought when she turned the corner of the greenhouse and headed for the door. A hint of movement caught her attention in the trees behind the structure and she pulled up short so she could study the area. She stared so long without seeing anything she almost convinced herself she imagined it. Then she saw a flutter of fabric. It looked like the edge of a cape.

"Hello?"

No one answered.

"Hello?" Ivy took a hesitant step forward. For some reason – and she had no idea why – she could feel someone staring at her. She considered walking into the woods and confronting the individual, but she knew that would be a bad move given the circumstances. Instead she reached into her pocket to retrieve her phone – she had every intention of calling Jack for backup – but it became unnecessary when a small figure hopped out of the trees.

Ivy jolted and then sighed when she realized who she was looking at. "Brandon McKay! What are you doing?"

The small boy flashed a sheepish grin when he caught Ivy looking at him. "I wasn't doing nothing."

"You were obviously doing something," Ivy argued, striding forward and grabbing his hand. "Do you want to tell me what it is that you weren't doing?"

"I … no." Brandon shook his head.

Ivy cocked a challenging eyebrow. "You know I'm very tight with a police officer, right?" She knelt down so she was on eye-level with the child. "I'll make him lock you up if you don't tell me what you were doing." Ivy wasn't generally a fan of threatening children, but Brandon's reputation was something straight out of a nightmare. He'd retired more teachers than contract negotiations in Shadow Lake. Er, well, that was the rumor anyway.

"Would he really put me in jail?" Brandon didn't look convinced.

"He would if I asked him to do it," Ivy replied. "I happen to know you guys were warned to stay away from the trees. You either need to tell me what you were doing or I'm going to get my friend the police officer and you're going to have to tell him."

"But … ." Brandon made a face. "Fine. Do you really want to know?"

Given the way he phrased the question, Ivy couldn't help but rethink her demand. Ultimately, though, she knew she had to stick to her guns. "Yes."

"Here." Brandon held out his hand and Ivy realized he was holding a clump of dirt.

"Why do you have that?" Ivy asked, shrinking away. She had no idea if he had something else in there, but she wasn't keen to find out. "That's not a dead animal or anything, is it?"

"It's just dirt," Brandon answered. "I'm going to rub it on my sister's head. She's dressed up like a princess and I'm sick of her asking everyone to tell her how pretty she looks."

"Well, that's a girl thing," Ivy said, reining in her temper. "Just ignore her."

"I would rather throw dirt at her."

"Well, you're not going to do that," Ivy said. "I'll have Jack arrest you if you do."

"Really? He's going to arrest me for throwing dirt?" Brandon was understandably dubious.

"I just told you he would do what I asked," Ivy said, grabbing the boy's elbow and directing him toward the trees. "Dump it in there ... and wipe your hands on your pants."

"Mom said never to do that."

"Well, you have her take it up with me if she has a problem," Ivy said. "I ... ." She didn't get a chance to finish because another figure – this one much bigger – barreled out of the woods and grabbed her arms, snapping her head back and momentarily stunning her.

Brandon was so surprised he dropped his treasured dirt and took an involuntarily step back, gasping out a frightened squeak as he stared at the man.

"What the ... ?" Ivy couldn't make out any features because the man was wearing a grotesque clown mask. Even though his hands were on her, she remained convinced it was a Halloween prank. That feeling only lasted a second when she had a brief flash that made it appear she was looking at herself. That's when she realized she was in a lot more trouble than she initially envisioned.

"Is that the police?" Brandon asked, her voice ratcheting up a notch. "Is he going to put me in jail? I dropped the dirt."

Ivy struggled to fight off the man as he attempted to drag her into the woods. She was torn between wanting to keep Brandon safe and worrying about her own wellbeing. Finally, she did the only thing she could do. "Run, Brandon! He's a bad man."

"But … ." Brandon's eyes filled with tears as Ivy cried out, the stranger bending her wrist back as he tried to gain control of her flailing arms.

"Run!" Ivy yelled, the sound immediately being drowned out by screaming children inside of the guesthouse. "Find the police officer. Run!"

Brandon didn't wait to be told again. He turned on his heel and fled toward the front of the greenhouse as Ivy continued to struggle against her assailant. Even though she put up a tremendous fight, he was still too strong for her. Before she realized what was happening, she was pulled into the woods and away from the safety her heart desperately needed.

Jack!

HOW about that one?" Max looked the blonde Wonder Woman up and down. "I think I would like to see if she has a magic lasso."

Jack had long ago lost interest in the game. "She's perfect," he said, pushing himself away from the tree. "Go forth and … let her tie you down with her magic lasso. Wow. There's a sentence I never thought I would say."

"Feels good, doesn't it?"

"Not particularly," Jack replied. "I don't really care who you end up with for the night, though. I want to find my witch and get in some spells."

"Ugh. You're so gross."

"I do my best." Jack moved to walk away from Max but stilled when he saw a small boy in a cape – his hands filthy, as if he'd been digging in dirt – standing two feet away. His hand was shaking as he pressed it to his mouth and his eyes were flooded with tears. "What's wrong, buddy?"

"I ... ."

"That's Brandon," Max said, dragging his attention away from Wonder Woman and focusing on the boy as he stepped closer. "He's a pile of trouble from everything I've heard."

"He doesn't look like he's getting in trouble," Jack said, shuffling closer to the boy. "You're not getting in trouble, are you?"

Brandon shook his head as a tear slipped down his cheek. "I was getting in trouble, but ... Miss Ivy found me and told me to put the dirt back."

"Miss Ivy, huh?" Jack couldn't help but smile. "Did she tell on you?"

Brandon shook his head. "She said she was going to tell you to arrest me if I didn't admit what I was doing. I told her and then ... ."

"And then what?"

Brandon's voice was barely a whisper. "And then a bad clown came out of the woods and grabbed her."

Jack's stomach flipped. "What do you mean?" He wasn't sure if he should believe the boy. It was a night of costumes and screams. He could've misunderstood something he saw.

"The clown jumped out of the trees," Brandon said. "Miss Ivy hit him and tried to get away, but she couldn't. She told me to run and find you."

Jack was instantly alert as he craned his neck and searched for a glimpse of Ivy. He came up short. "Where, Brandon? You need to show me where."

"Behind the greenhouse."

Jack nodded and kept his grim smile in place as he patted the boy's head. "Max, find your father and whatever men you can get and then head into the woods. Spread out in groups of two."

"What are you going to do?" All thought of running off with Wonder Woman fled Max's mind the moment he realized his sister was in danger.

"I'm going to find Ivy," Jack said brightly, putting on a show for Brandon's benefit before lowering his voice so only Max could hear. "And then I'm going to kill whoever would dare touch her. If she's hurt ... I swear ... I will end whoever this is."

"WHO ARE you?"

Ivy rubbed her wrist as she rested her back against a tree. She knew the woods behind her house better than anyone, but she'd lost her sense of direction in the darkness. She couldn't be sure exactly where she was.

After grabbing her by the greenhouse, her assailant dragged her through the trees. She opened her mouth to scream at one point – convinced it was her only shot before he forced her away from the nursery grounds – but the man realized what she was going to do a split-second before she did it and clamped his hand over her mouth. All she managed was a small squeak.

The man stood about three feet away, his chest heaving as he glared at her. They walked at least a quarter of a mile in the dark. In the grand scheme of things, that wasn't very far. Given the fact that Ivy was separated from everyone, though, it felt like a continent divided her from Jack.

"Don't you know?" The man hadn't spoken since grabbing her, so when he finally opened his mouth, Ivy was surprised.

"Why should I know?" Ivy asked. "You're wearing a mask."

"You're psychic or something, though," the man replied. "You see things. You saw inside of my head."

Ivy wet her lips as she glanced around. The forest was eerily silent. If Jack was out searching for her she was certain he would make noise during the endeavor. He had no idea where she was, though. He was searching blindly in the dark. The odds of him finding her … .

"Aren't you going to answer me?" The man adopted a taunting tone and drew Ivy's blue eyes to his face. "Aren't you going to tell me how you managed to crawl inside of my head?"

"Not until you tell me who you are."

"And why would I want to do that?"

Ivy shrugged. "I don't know," she answered. "Perhaps you want to do it because you know this is your big chance to gloat. That's the reason the killer reveals his identity in books and movies. We could treat it like a *Scooby-Doo* episode. That might be fun."

Instead of laughing – or smacking her, which Ivy thought was a legitimate possibility – the man tilted his head to the side and studied her through the rubber clown mask's eyeholes. It was a disturbing sight under the muted light.

"Who are you?" Ivy repeated, her heart rate escalating. She knew she should recognize the man, but it was as if she had a mental block. There was something so familiar about him … .

"Do you really want to know?"

Ivy bit her lip and nodded.

"Okay, but you asked for it." The man reached for the back of the mask and pulled it over his face.

At first all Ivy could see was a mess of brown hair. Then, as he slowly lifted his chin, the features became clear. "Brad?" Of all the people Ivy envisioned being responsible for Jeff Johnson's death, Brad Gardner was the last face she expected to see.

"Oh, what? Are you surprised?" Brad mocked, tossing the mask on the ground and smoothing his hair. "You've been in my head. How come you didn't know it was me?"

Ivy had no idea how to respond. Technically, she had been in his head. She'd never been in there long enough to sniff out an identity, tough. "I didn't purposely do that," she said, choosing her words carefully. "It just happened."

"Oh, it just happened? How did it just happen?"

"I have no idea," Ivy answered honestly. "The first time it kind of happened was the day we discovered Jeff's body in the maze. I touched his shoe and … went to a different place."

Brad knit his eyebrows together. "Like where? Did you go to Hell or something?"

"It doesn't really work like that," Ivy explained. "It's more like I went into a memory – or perhaps an echo of Jeff's last moments. I didn't see you, though. I didn't feel you. I felt his pain. I think that's what the burning sensation was anyway. I heard him crying, too. He didn't want to die."

"It's kind of funny that you say that, because those were his last words," Brad said, chuckling harshly. "He kept whimpering like a baby. *I don't want to die. I don't want to die.* He had to die, though."

Ivy felt sick to her stomach thanks to Brad's callous words. He was clearly a sociopath – and maybe even worse. He had no remorse for what he'd done. He almost looked as if he enjoyed doing it. "Why did he have to die?"

"Because I needed it to happen," Brad answered. "Forget about that for a second. Go back to you and your ... ability ... to climb into my head. How did you do it?"

Ivy was frustrated by Brad's refusal to give her a motive and his insistence that she could somehow control her newfound ability. "I don't know how it happened. It just happened."

"I felt you there," Brad said. "I felt you crawling inside of my head. Did you know that would happen?"

"No."

"Well, it did," Brad snapped. "You were inside of my head and I wanted to scream. I could feel you in there ... it was as if you were trying to crawl your way out."

"But how did you know it was me?" Ivy challenged. "I didn't know I was seeing through your eyes."

"Because I could hear people talking to you," Brad answered. "That day Jack and Brian came to the firehouse, I thought for sure they were there to arrest me. I had a dream earlier that day. I was killing Jeff all over again and you were watching.

"For some reason I knew it was really happening, though, and I still don't understand why," he continued. "I could hear Jack screaming for you. He was yelling your name. I later heard from people in town that you passed out when you saw Jeff's body. Maisie said all of that really happened. That's how I knew it wasn't a dream.

"I knew then that I was in trouble," he said. "Then it happened again that day out here. You were sitting in the woods and I was going to ask you about the dream. I watched you for a full day before then. I was hoping to be able to talk to you away from everyone else, but you were never alone. Well, you weren't alone until you took off into the trees that one day. I was going to approach you then, but then I had this ... flash ... and I was in your spot looking forward. It confused me and I lost my chance because you took off into the woods."

"I saw you the day you attacked Don Merriman in his garage, too," Ivy said.

"Oh, I know," Brad intoned. "You're the reason he's still alive. You're the reason this entire plan is probably going to fall apart. You're the reason I'm going to have to find a way inside of the hospital to kill him when no one is looking. That's after I kill you first, though, of course. There can be no loose ends. My ... friend ... won't stand for it."

Ivy's heart rolled at the words and she clenched her hands on top of her knees. "W-what?"

"Oh, you didn't think I was alone, did you?" Brian barked out a demented laugh. "Oh, that's cute. You did think I was alone in this. I guess you're not as smart as you thought, huh?"

Ivy had no idea what he was talking about until another figure emerged from the shadows. She wasn't expecting this face either, and when it popped into view, everything in her head tilted.

"No way."

Twenty-Three

"Why is she still alive?"

Karen Johnson kept one hand on her huge stomach and the other on her lower back as she glared at Brad. He didn't seem surprised by her appearance, but Ivy felt as if her head was mired in quicksand as she attempted to wrap her mind around the new wrinkle.

"I wanted to ask her a few questions," Brad growled. "I want to know how she's been getting into my head."

"I told you that was crap," Karen snapped. "You're imagining it because you're feeling guilty or something. Calm down."

"I'm not imagining it," Brad said. "She just admitted to being able to do it. Tell her, Ivy."

Ivy licked her lips. "Um … ."

"Yeah, I think he's crazy, too," Karen said. "If he's trying to get you to admit that, go ahead and ignore him. I think he has residual guilt about killing Jeff or something. It's making him a bit wonky."

Ivy couldn't help but wonder if she wasn't the one going around the bend. "But … what are you doing here, Karen?"

"Oh, geez, really?" Karen rolled her eyes. "Do you really want an explanation?"

"She was in my head," Brad seethed.

Karen ignored him. "I guess you deserve it," she said. "I am sorry about having to kill you, but we don't really have a choice. Brad won't let this whole 'she's eating my brain' thing go. It's so annoying."

Karen spoke as if she didn't have a care in the world, which only served to baffle Ivy even more.

"Brad and I are together," Karen explained. "We've been together for over a year now. We're going to run away from this hellhole town as soon as we can and build a life together. We obviously have to wait until people won't be surprised by our relationship, but we've got it all planned out."

"But ... what about Jeff?"

"What about him?" Karen challenged. "Do you think that Maisie was the first woman he stepped out with while he was married to me? Don't kid yourself. Jeff cheated on me every chance he got. Most of the time it was women he met at out-of-town bars, and he was only with them for a night, but I knew. He actually brought gonorrhea home once. He tried to tell me he caught it from a toilet seat. Can you believe that?"

There was a lot about this situation Ivy couldn't believe. That was the least jarring part of it, though. "If he was cheating on you, why not just leave him?"

"Because I have no money or job skills and I didn't have any options," Karen replied. "That all changed when Brad and I hooked up. We started dreaming together and we figured out a way where we could get everything – including Jeff's life insurance policy – so that's what we decided to do."

Things clicked into place for Ivy. It was still a sordid tale, but she understood it much better. "You lucked out when Jeff was so open about his relationship with Maisie, huh?"

"I really did," Karen said. "Everyone knew he was cheating on me. Maisie made a perfect scapegoat. We had to make sure to kill Jeff when I was so big no one could ever believe I had a part in it, of course. That made us move up our timetable a bit.

"I was hoping she would get arrested for the murder, but that didn't happen because Brad decided to get fancy," she continued. "I told him to dump Jeff's body in the Halloween display. Maisie was in and out of that thing for days and I knew she would be drawn into the investigation. I didn't tell him to put it on the cross, though. He did that himself."

"I thought it was cooler," Brad protested.

"But that's how the police knew it was a man who killed Jeff," Ivy said, her mind busy. "A woman wouldn't have the upper body strength to hoist him up there."

"Exactly," Karen intoned. "See, Brad. She gets it. Why don't you?" Karen talked down to Brad as if he was a small child. He didn't seem upset by her tone, though, which made Ivy realize it wasn't a new thing. "Now we're kind of stuck because Maisie can't be a suspect and we need someone else to take the fall for Jeff's death."

"But … what about your father?"

"He was supposed to be the next scapegoat," Karen said. "We were going to blame him and fake a suicide. He saw Brad, though, and he tried to run. Brad had no choice but to attack him. We couldn't really pretend it was a suicide after that."

"He's your father, though," Ivy said. "How could you kill your own father?"

"You've met him," Karen said. "He's a jerk. He's always been a jerk. He's never cared about me. The only reason he's been hanging around now is because he wants a piece of the life insurance payout. Of course, I have to get the payout for that to happen."

"The insurance company won't release the funds until you've been cleared in Jeff's death," Ivy surmised. "That won't happen until someone else has been arrested and charged."

"And convicted," Karen said. "I was hoping that faking my father's suicide would cut through all of that messy red tape. He's still alive, though."

"Just until I can get into the hospital," Brad said. "I'll make it look like a suicide, baby. I swear."

"How is that going to work?" Ivy challenged. "He clearly didn't attack himself in the garage. People know that."

"Yes, but we're going to make sure Dave Johnson goes down for that," Karen said. "He's always hated my father. People will believe he went after my father as some form of payback because he believes my father killed Jeff.

"See, we're going to set it up so that it looks like Dad killed Jeff and Dave went after Dad as revenge," she continued. "It's pretty much foolproof. Well, except for you. I have no idea how we're going to explain you. Brad refuses to move forward until you're out of the picture, though. He thinks you're haunting him."

"She is!" Brad was beside himself. "Tell her you've been in my head, Ivy."

Ivy decided to lie on the spot. "I have no idea what you're talking about."

"I told you," Karen said, puffing out her chest in a haughty manner. "You imagined it. Now she has to die for nothing. She had no idea it was you."

"You don't have to kill me," Ivy suggested. "You can just leave me out here – maybe tie me to a tree or something – and make your getaway."

"I would love to do that because I genuinely like you, but it's not possible," Karen said. "We can't leave town until I have the life insurance money. That's weeks – if not months – away. Plus, I'm going to pop out this kid any day now. That really cuts down on our traveling options."

The baby. Something occurred to Ivy when she thought about the baby. "The baby is Brad's, isn't it?"

Karen nodded. "Jeff and I barely had sex. He had way too much of it with other people. Still, when I realized I was pregnant, I had to sleep with him again to buy time. That really sucked, by the way. I had to get him drunk and everything."

"It sounds horrible," Ivy deadpanned, rolling her neck until it cracked. Her butt was starting to go numb from the cold ground beneath her. "How did you even get this far out in the woods in your condition?"

"Far?" Karen made a face. "The road is right there."

Ivy followed the direction she pointed with her eyes. It took her a moment to realize they'd traveled much farther east than she realized. The road that led to the nursery was right there … which meant the parking lot was probably only a quarter of a mile away. If she could get to her feet and run … .

"I won't say anything," Ivy promised, dragging her eyes back to Karen. "Please don't kill me. I don't want to die."

The simple declaration triggered something in Brad … and it wasn't good. "Don't say that, you witch! I told you that's what Jeff said right before I killed him. I don't ever want to hear that again."

He waved his knife around for emphasis and Karen grabbed his wrist to make sure he didn't inadvertently catch her with the tip.

"Calm down," Karen soothed. "She's just trying to rattle you. Take a deep breath. We're almost out of this. It will just be another minute or two and then we can go. I promise everything is going to be okay."

"But she's lying," Brad said. "She has been in my head. Tell her you're lying, Ivy!" When Brad swiveled, he found Ivy was on her feet and moving away from the tree. She was quick and silent with her movements, and the realization that she was running away from him was almost too much for Brad's fragile mind to bear. "Ivy!"

"Get her!" Karen screeched. "She'll ruin everything if she gets away."

Brad crashed through the trees as he followed Ivy. It wasn't easy for her to run in the dress, but ironically enough, the slit made it so she could pump her legs without risk of tripping. She kicked off her shoes so she could increase her pace without slipping or sliding. She felt the cold seeping into the soles of her feet – along with a million hard edges and branches – but she pushed the pain out of her mind as she raced for the clearing on the other side of the trees. She was almost to the open air, where she was convinced someone would see her, when an arm snaked out from the last row of trees and grabbed her.

Ivy lashed out, slapping the hand away. She opened her mouth to scream, Jack's name on the tip of her tongue, but a hand clasped the back of her head and Jack's mouth covered hers in an effort to silence her.

"It's me, honey," he whispered, holding her up as she sagged against him. "I have you. I … love you."

Ivy heard the words but barely registered them as she gripped the front of Jack's costume. "It's Brad and Karen. He's coming."

"I hear him," Jack soothed, pushing Ivy behind him. "Stay here a second."

"But … ."

"Stay here," Jack repeated. He remained calm as he hid in the shadows.

Brad made a ton of noise as he barreled through the trees, causing Ivy to shrink back as he grew closer. Jack waited until the exact right moment and then he extended his arm, clotheslining Brad and causing him to gasp as he flew back in the other direction.

Jack was quick as he moved forward, pressing his foot to Brad's wrist and making sure the knife could go nowhere as he leveled his gun on the disoriented firefighter and pursed his lips. It took Brad a moment to realize what happened.

"You," Brad muttered. "How did you find us?"

"It wasn't hard," Jack replied. "I simply followed my heart."

"I don't know what that means."

"Of course you don't," Jack said. "You don't understand what it means to love someone."

The sound of voices on the road caught Ivy's attention and she hurried in that direction, waving her arms when she caught sight of Brian flashing a light into the trees. "Down here! Jack has him. Come quick."

Brian broke into a run when he saw her, giving Ivy a cursory once-over before hurrying to his partner's side.

He widened his eyes when he realized exactly who Jack had on the ground. "Seriously?"

"It gets worse," Ivy volunteered. "Karen is in the woods. She's his partner and the baby is his."

"I … ." Brian worked his jaw and then nodded. "Okay. We've got this. Ivy, go down to the nursery. Your father and Max are about to have a fit. We'll handle this and then … well, I have no idea what. It's definitely going to be a long night, though."

Ivy cast a worried look at Jack. The last thing she wanted to do was leave him.

"Go, honey," Jack prodded. "You're cold and need to warm up. I'll be there as soon as I can."

"Do you promise?"

"I promise."

MAX poured two mugs of hot chocolate into Ivy and wrapped her feet in his gym socks – which she did not appreciate – before Jack made his way back to the nursery an hour later. After news spread about what happened in the woods, everyone packed up their kids and left. The only ones remaining were Max, Michael, and Ivy.

The second Ivy saw Jack, she broke away from Max and raced toward him. She threw her arms around his neck and relished the way he tugged her to him. He lifted her off the ground as he petted the back of her head and locked gazes with Michael.

"Thank you for watching her."

"She's my daughter," Michael said. "I think that's my job."

"Well, I'm going to relieve you of your duty for the rest of the night."

Michael widened his eyes. "Don't you have to go into the station?"

"Brian is handling it," Jack replied, refusing to relinquish his grip on Ivy. "We're not going to question them until tomorrow, so I actually have plenty of time. I just want some time alone with Ivy, if that's okay, I mean."

"I understand," Michael said, smiling. "She's been a real pain since being separated from you. We tried to get her to go back to the house, but she refused. She wanted to be close and knew you would come here first."

"That's why she's my girl," Jack said, smiling as he rubbed his cheek against Ivy's soft skin and not speaking again until Max and Michael were out of earshot. "Are you okay?"

"I'm fine," Ivy said. "He didn't touch me other than to drag me through the woods. He took such a weird trek I kind of got lost."

"Well, thankfully for you, he wasn't good about covering his tracks," Jack said. "I saw his car hidden in the trees. I played a hunch that he would come out of the woods there. I guess it paid off."

"I guess so." Ivy pressed her eyes shut as she basked in Jack's warmth. The night air was cold, but she didn't care. "Thank you for coming after me."

"I love you, Ivy," Jack said. "I will always find a way to you."

Ivy sucked in a breath at the words. She heard him when he was by the trees, but it didn't sink in until they were separated. She couldn't believe he was saying it twice in one night. "I love you, too."

"I know you do," Jack said, rocking her gently. "I'm sorry this happened at your favorite time of year. Now you're probably going to have bad memories."

"No. Now I have the best memory ever thanks to you. I wasn't sure if you felt that way and then ... ."

"Oh, honey, I've felt that way since the beginning," Jack said, pulling his head back so he could stare into her eyes. "I worried you didn't feel it either. Looking at you now, that was stupid. I guess we were stupid together, huh?"

"I like to think of myself as a genius."

Jack chuckled. "That's because you're an amazing woman," he said, pressing a soft kiss to her mouth. "Do you want to go home?"

Ivy nodded. "We can celebrate our love."

Jack grinned. "That sounds like the best thing ever."

"But ... what about Brad and Karen?" Ivy was torn. "Do you have all of the answers you need?"

"Karen pretty much owned up to everything because she wants to cut a deal and blame Brad," Jack replied. "This whole thing is going to take some time to sort out. It's not going to happen tonight, though. Tonight is for you and me."

"Are you sure?"

"Honey, I've never been more sure of anything in my entire life," Jack said. "I love you. I want to be with you. We'll leave the rest of the world until tomorrow."

"You had me at love."

"We both have each other to love," Jack clarified. "Nothing is going to change that ... and I refuse to be afraid to say what's in my heart. From now on, I'm going to tell everyone I see that I love you."

Ivy giggled. "That sounds nice."

"Good," Jack said, hoisting her up so she had no choice but to wrap her legs around his waist. "Let's go be in love, shall we?"

"And that's why this is still my favorite time of year."

"Mine, too, honey. Mine, too."

Ivy still had no idea if the new ability was tied to the Blood Moon or if it was something that would fade now that Brad was in custody, but she found she didn't have the energy to worry about it. Jack loved her. She loved him. They were in love with each other. That was the most important thing.

Jack was right. The rest could be dealt with at a later time. For now, all they needed was each other.

57831565R00144

Made in the USA
Lexington, KY
26 November 2016